KEY IN LOCK

Also by Rona Altrows

A Run On Hose

Nov. 2 2010
Thanks so much
for coming, Shirley.
Hope you enjoy
my little
stories.
xo
Rona

KEY IN LOCK

RONA ALTROWS

RECLINER BOOKS

Copyright © Rona Altrows, 2010
All rights reserved
No part of this publication may be reproduced or transmitted in any form or by any means, graphic, electronic or mechanical, including photocopying, recording, or any information storage and retrieval system, without permission in writing from the publisher or a licence from The Canadian Copyright Licensing Agency (Access Copyright). For an Access Copyright licence, visit www.accesscopyright.ca or call toll free to 1-800-893-5777.

Library and Archives Canada Cataloguing in Publication
Altrows, Rona
Key in lock / Rona Altrows.
Short stories.

ISBN 978-0-9813640-4-9

I. Title.

PS8601.L86K49 2010 C813'.6 C2010-905956-5

Key in Lock is a work of fiction.

The author gratefully acknowledges the financial support of the Canada Council for the Arts and Alberta Foundation for the Arts through the Alberta Creative Development Grant.

Canada Council for the Arts Conseil des Arts du Canada

Edited by Dustin Smith

Cover image: Gabriel von Max, *Woman in Contemplation (Sinnende)*, c. 1880, The Daulton Collection.

Printed and bound in Canada on acid-free paper.

Recliner Books
PO Box 64128
5512 4 Street NW
Calgary, AB, T2K 1A9
www.ReclinerBooks.com

For Bill

Contents

Key In Lock

A MAN NEEDS A certain amount of intercourse. You can stay at the rubbing-pressing-groping stage for only so long. You may be able to stretch it out for months, which is how it's been going with Raymond and me. When you are in your sixties, like we are, you like to extend everything out, move at a more relaxed pace, as though that will convince the Grim Reaper not to rush.

It's not as if he's said so in words, but through the way he acts, Raymond has shown me how he would like the scene to unfold; he'll be ready any time I am. And to be fair to him, I can't hold out forever. I mean, he has been patient, a gentleman—no pushing or insisting. But at some point, no matter how sweet a guy is, or how old, only penetration will do. I'm in a jam now. He's great company, a fine man, and easy on the eyes, but I'll never love him. What's more—and this is the part that scares me right now—there's something I don't want him to know. If we keep seeing each other, there's a chance he'll learn my secret; if we go all the way, he'll find out for sure. Can I live with that?

So I've given myself a deadline. Tonight. We're going

out to a movie, and then he'll drive me back to my apartment for a drink. By then, I'll have made up my mind. Right now I'm still doing the back and forth.

We humans would probably be better off if we were built more like banana slugs. In her university classes, my young friend Julie learns how animals go about their business. She knows I am curious and tells me the juiciest stuff, like the slugs' story. She talks about how they court for hours, which is like years for them, and how they snack on each other's slime before sex. But to me, the best part is the location of the genitals, not too far from the head. With that anatomy, I figure there's a good chance that they use their heads when it comes to deciding about sex. Not like us. All that distance between the brain and the other place leads to nothing but trouble. Bad matches, heartache, aggravation—I'll bet those are not major problems among the slugs.

And there's another thing slugs have got on us—mucus. In slug sex, there is an exchange of mucus, which is what I will need more of if I am going to take that next step with Raymond. Not mucus exactly, but lubricant. After a person goes through the change, those juices just don't flow as easily as before. For the first few years after my periods stopped I hardly noticed, because the memory of my husband Henry was still at the top of my mind, even though he had died years before. For a long time, I refused to concentrate on anything happening in that part of my body. But two years ago I was cured of the kind of grief that holds a person back. I know how to pleasure myself; I learned how to do it from books I took out of the public library. By trying out some of the suggestions, I rediscovered a part of myself that I had put in cold storage for eighteen years. Then men started to look better too. *That* way, I mean. So I started dating, and now, at sixty-two, I have come to understand one basic fact about sex in the second half of life: you need extra moisture.

Fine, so you make sure you've got lubricating jelly in your medicine cabinet. But what if you pee at the wrong time? You're supposed to achieve bladder control in early childhood, yet here I am, a grown woman, with a leaky faucet. Of course, some of my older customers at Marjorie's Lingerie have trouble holding their water because of one health condition or another. They tell me about the problem and I comfort them. "It's just the bratty human body doing things its own way," I say to them. But secretly, I always believed that I personally was not the incontinence type. Now that I know I am, I'm using a double standard. All other women are allowed to dribble off cue. Just not me. And I sure don't want any guy I am dating to see me spring a leak. Not Raymond and not anyone who comes after. Maybe I will just have to give up sex, period.

Dr. Wexler reminds me to do my Kegels, which are exercises for the floor of the pelvis. Spare embarrassment by learning to control the urge. Do fifty to a hundred repetitions a day. Suck in vagina and rectum, hold, release. Hold to a count of ten to develop strength; perform short snappers to build up speed. "In case the urge hits you while you are at one end of the mall and the public washrooms are at the other," Dr. Wexler says. Well, I don't spend too much time in shopping malls, but those Kegels serve me well wherever I do find myself—in a fitting room at Marjorie's Lingerie; in the elevator of my dentist's office; on the walking path by the river. My secret exercises are invisible to the outside world and always available to me. I can do them while sitting in a movie theatre or balancing my bankbook. No equipment required. Good old Kegels. People do them in public all the time. I may think the woman standing next to me at the bus stop is staring blankly into space. Wrong. She is doing her Kegels.

Dr. Wexler says what I've got is sometimes called key in lock syndrome. You're out and about, you need to pee, you head home, you reach the front door and you know you're so close to relief, to comfort. You insert your key in the lock and let your guard down, and that's when you're in real trouble. The urinary urgency becomes so strong, you may not reach the bathroom on time. One Sunday last August, I didn't make it—had to plop my bum down on the lawn of my apartment building, pretend to be sun-tanning, and let the flood come. Nobody was around to see but that didn't help. I sat in shame. When I got home I unplugged the phone and cried all through my shower and the underwear laundering. I did not prepare lunch and it wasn't from lack of hunger. I purposely denied myself that meal. Maybe it wasn't the most mature response but I just didn't know how to react to the bad behaviour of my own body. I was angry at it for betraying me and wanted to punish it.

After that I thought, okay, we are not going to have another fake sun-tanning experience. Ever. Kegels or no Kegels, I was going to make sure that if a leak sprouted against my will, I would protect myself against humiliation. It was time for a trip to the pharmacy. I took the bus all the way to Oakridge, which is a part of town I don't normally have occasion to go to, and found a nice big impersonal drug store. I looked around slowly, methodically, as though I were conducting an inventory, and soon enough I found the overhead sign I wanted: AISLE 13: FIRST AID, FEMALE HYGIENE, INCONTENCE. *Incontence?* I knew I should ask to speak to the manager. After all, I run a store too, and the last thing we need is a badly spelled sign. I know my customers; they are sensitive to quality control. It would offend them to read about a sale on *camsioles*. They want their undergarments to be attractive, well-made and accurately spelled. And they'd be just as upset, maybe even more so, to read that *Incontence* sign in the pharmacy. If I can help a fellow retailer, I always feel it's worth the few minutes it takes out of my day to do it. That's why, a couple of months back, I told Jason, the owner of the Bean Wave, that his poster was advertising *Fresh Rosted Coffee and Internet*. He had not caught the error and as soon as I pointed it out, he got on the phone to order a properly spelled replacement poster. He thanked me with a hug and a five dollar Bean

Wave gift certificate. Spelling was one of my best subjects in school.

But as I started looking for the pharmacy manager, I asked myself, did I really want that person to know that I was the one who discovered the spelling mistake on his overhead aisle sign? What if the manager was a man? I especially dread having men know about this problem of mine; that's why I am putting myself through all this misery over Raymond. Would the male manager ask me if I needed some assistance in finding the correct incontinence product? Maybe it would be like when you ask for help in the supermarket, because you can't find the salsa, and the clerk walks down the aisle with you and asks which brand you want and what size. That's if you have a real keener of a clerk, a person like me, who loves to give good service. But here's the thing—I didn't want Mr. Keener Pharmacy Manager to get into those questions. *Thanks for the spelling tip, ma'am, and what kind of incontinence product can I offer you? The full brief or the napkin? Pads are available in a variety of styles, the super absorbent, the extra coverage panty liner and everything in between. We're running twenty percent off on the Confidence Pluses here; they're on promotion right now and have just gone to this new indigo-coloured packaging. Or how would you like to try out our house brand? High absorbency, good value.*

I bolted out of the pharmacy before that pitch could happen. As I power-walked down the block to the bus stop, I remembered Henry telling me about something that happened years before I met him. He was eighteen, with a sixteen-year-old girlfriend, and he drove down to a pharmacy to buy his first package of condoms. Like lots of other boys in that situation, he was too scared to face a cashier. He left empty-handed and his girlfriend kept her virtue, which was probably just as well.

My best friend Doreen and I have been through so much together in the years since we played on the same high school teams. I call and ask for her advice about Raymond, but I don't discuss the incontinence. I haven't brought myself to share that information, not even with Doreen. So in a way, it's not right for me to talk to her about Raymond. She doesn't have all the facts.

"Think about what you're doing, Irene," she says. "This guy really likes you."

"I like him too," I say. "Why else would I be seeing him?"

"I don't know," she says. "It may be best for you to cut him loose. You don't seem to feel the same way he does. I mean, you don't care for him that deeply, do you?"

"So what? Does every relationship need to reach as deep as the ocean floor? Isn't it enough that we're kind to each other and can enjoy a game of Scrabble or a show together?"

"No," Doreen says. "It's not enough and you know it, not if the other person has different ideas. If you don't have strong feelings for Raymond, you ought to think about dropping him. He wants to be your guy, not your buddy."

I need to figure this out before Raymond and I get together tonight and attraction gets in the way. I want to use my head, like a banana slug. It's not as if I don't find him attractive. And although I can't see staying with him forever, I do get pleasure from the cuddling and making out. Plus, I'll admit it to myself, I like the attention. True, I am keeping something very personal from him. But is it wrong not to tell a steady date absolutely everything? No matter how I look at my problem, from any angle, it comes down to this. If I get intimate with Raymond, he is bound to see something I want to keep private. And although I am fond of him, this is not love. If he found out, it would be a bit like sharing an intimacy with a casual friend, wouldn't it? Is that a wrong thing to do?

When he picks me up I still don't know what will happen. On the way over to the theatre, we make small talk. I'm uneasy but try not to show it. He seems to be relaxed, although I could easily be wrong. I don't read my dates as well as I read my customers. The movie turns out to be about nothing, except maybe Julia Roberts showing off her perfect teeth. We don't bother discussing it. Instead, Raymond brings up an even more annoying subject—how his daughter is still having trouble toilet training Caden, her three-year-old son. I don't mind hearing about Caden's tumbling skills in his toddler gymnastic class or his signs of musical genius on the kazoo or his strangely mature abstract paintings. But I always dread the next chapter of the potty saga. Pants-wetting talk is too close to home for me, although of course, Raymond has no way to know that. Not yet.

He tells me that his daughter read about a system called behaviour marks, something like that. Every time Caden went in the toilet, he got a reward, a gold star on the chart. After a while the stars lost their shine because of overuse, and he started protest-peeing on the floor. The mother switched to jelly bean rewards, one jelly bean for Caden after every successful trip to the toilet. But it turned out he was not that crazy about jelly beans, and lately she has had to practically shove them down his throat. Not such a rewarding reward. Again he is back-sliding in his toilet training. Back to Square One.

If she tore up the star chart and threw out the jelly beans, she'd have better luck—that's what I think. Leave the kid alone and eventually he will find his own way to the bathroom at the right times. He won't be wetting his jeans as a grown man, will he? Somehow, he will learn.

I don't share those thoughts with Raymond. After over thirty-two years in customer service, I've learned something about people's preferences. They prefer not to be criticized on how they are raising their kids, or on how their grown kids are raising the grandchildren. Anyway, since I have never had kids of my own, who am I to comment?

"Boys are always slower," Raymond says. I know that's not true, because Doreen's daughter Toni was not fully trained until she was five years old, and continued to wet the bed from time to time right into her early teens. But I hold my tongue.

Once he has expressed whatever he needs to about Caden, I speak. "We need to talk about us," I say. It's a weary line, but how else does a person put it?

He looks worried. There's not much conversation for the rest of the car ride.

Back at my apartment, I get a beer out of the fridge and bring it to him. "Aren't you going to have your glass of white wine?" he asks.

"I'm not thirsty."

When something miserable needs to be done—the bills need paying, say, or the toilet needs scrubbing—I try to get on with it as soon as I can. Thinking about the chore feels worse than doing it. The perfect moment will never arrive. Once Raymond has gotten a start on his beer, I jump in.

"I don't feel as though we're going anywhere," I say.

For long seconds, we sit in silence. Then he asks, "Where would you like us to go?"

We talk. If he wants to ride into the sunset with me, he isn't saying so, and I don't blame him. Why should he expose himself completely, when he sees I don't feel the same way? He tells me he feels no need to make plans; let's just enjoy the present. But his eyes don't agree with his words. He doesn't want the axe to drop. The more he stresses the joy of the moment and all that, the more I realize that Doreen is right. It would be unfair of me to go on dating this man. I won't spell out what he hasn't got. Even if I tried to go that route, I wouldn't know what to say. Any effort to explain would make him feel worse. What would that accomplish?

As we talk, I think about my fear of his discovering the key-in-lock problem. Now he won't. Why am I not relieved?

An hour later, we are officially no longer on our way to becoming a couple. He is unhappy but he is carrying himself with dignity, like the gentleman he is.

"Would you like to be friends then?" he asks. "I'd value you very highly as a friend."

I'd better not agree to that. I'm pretty sure he would secretly always want the switcheroo back to romance, and that wouldn't be healthy for him.

"I don't think so," I say, "I am more of a clean-break sort of person."

"Fair enough," he says, and once again I am grateful that he is respecting my choice. But part of me wishes he would fight for me.

* * *

I've surprised myself by missing Raymond, even though it has already been a couple of months since the breakup. It's not a desperate kind of missing, like what I had after Henry died. It's low-key, more irritating than painful, like having a song that's not your favourite stuck in your head. I am prone to mental wanderings and I start having a repeating daydream. Raymond and I are lying in his bed. We have sex that is not earth-shaking but slow and slug-like, with lots of natural moisture. As soon as we are done I feel a pressing need to pee, and I run naked toward the ensuite bathroom and as I step over the threshold I lose bladder control and on comes the gush and then the shame. But what about Raymond? He's not uttering a sound. He's up there on the bed and I am facing the toilet. I have to know how he's taking this, have to see his reaction, it's all that matters. I try to turn my head but it's no use, I can't move it. My neck has locked up.

Down Low

CAN I ASK WHO it is?"

"I don't know, Gwen. I should consult the person first."

"Cut the crap, Trevor. See this condom in its shiny wrapper? I didn't conjure it out of thin air. It fell out of your pocket, just like in the cheesy movies."

I've been on the pill for the last thirteen years, so I know the salami slings are not for home use. He's just returned from a business trip. The evidence is mounting, and I will not stop asking what gives until he spills the truth.

More questions. Finally, he relents.

"Okay. Okay. All right. It's Phil Sterling."

"Phil? From your office?"

He says nothing.

I giggle softly, then a little louder, until I am splitting my sides, like a person who has slowly caught on to a killer joke. Trevor the shrimp and massive Phil—the mental picture of them in bed cracks me up. I mean, they look like they belong to two unrelated species. I laugh so hard that my breathing gets laboured and I need to gulp for air, and even when I no longer find anything funny, the laughter continues, as though it were a creature independent of me.

He sits. Waits.

I recover my equilibrium enough to go silent, but the parade of images continues. Trevor and me strolling hand in hand along Kensington Road on a fine summer afternoon—the petite blonde and her equally small dark-haired boyfriend. Strangers smile at us, like in a fifties film where the mere sight of a couple brightens the mood of every passerby. We could be the subject of an impressionist painting or an art photo like the "The Kiss." Young people in love in twentieth century Paris; middle-aged couple in love in twenty-first century Calgary; same uplifting effect on all who cross their path. We are in a special class, a couple whose friends refer to us as a unity. Trevorandgwen.

Not ready to think, I move on to the next picture. Whoops, not what I want. Leviathan Phil and minnow Trevor getting it on. This time I'm not amused, but an involuntary giggle comes out anyway.

"Are you done?" Trevor asks.

"Yes," I say.

"I wish I could laugh," he says.

Typical Trevor twist. Like I'm the insensitive one here.

For a few seconds we don't talk. I scramble to get past the emotional numbness that has seized me. But all I get is images of him and me, him and Phil Sterling. It's as though every part of me that can perceive, except for the visual, is in suspension. I am desperate to feel. Finally it comes. Something. It's nausea.

"Why him?" I ask. The words have come out without my permission. I don't really care why it's Phil in particular.

Silence.

"Look, can you do me a favour?" he says.

"*Now?*"

"Don't tell Paula Sterling. She has a heart condition. Phil says she could die of the shock."

"What is this, a soap opera? I've only ever seen the woman at your office Christmas parties. I'm not about to share confidences with her."

My wit stays sharp, my words come out with precision, but they are no part of me. The trouble is, I can be articulate under pressure. What I feel in the moment doesn't inhibit my ability to speak well and what I say doesn't necessarily correspond to what's going on inside me. This temperament hinders meaningful communication. I could be undergoing a leg amputation without anaesthetic and still converse coherently with the surgeon. On any subject.

"We'll get through this somehow," Trevor says. "I'll never leave you."

"Don't talk tripe."

The room reels. I run to the bathroom, vomit. After washing up, I set the lid onto the toilet and sit on it for a while, try to determine what I am experiencing. But it's no good; I can't make sense of the shards of feelings.

I flash back to a moment with my free-spirited friend

Alexa, during the delirium of our university days, when we cut late afternoon classes and sniffed out downtown bars for artistic looking boys. She called them wildflowers and they were for her plucking pleasure, not mine. I wasn't innocent, but neither did I require sexual contact with every seventeen to twenty-year-old male who made eye contact. Alexa did. I tagged along to keep her company and help identify wildflowers for her. Did I get any prurient pleasure out of our nature walks through the bars? Not consciously. On this day, Alexa hooked up with her most beautiful ever wildflower, a poet who told us nicely but clearly that he had a predilection for three-ways. He was an intelligent boy with high cheekbones and straight chestnut brown hair down to his ass, and he flirted with Alexa and me in equal measures. Somehow it arose in conversation that I was taking a course on the art and poetry of William Blake. He liked that. Once the preliminaries were done, we all walked back to Alexa's apartment and had a toke. I was already out of touch with myself and the grass only made it worse. Now I couldn't think lucidly either. Sensing my growing distance, the boy asked me if I knew Blake's painting *The Lovers' Whirlwind*, and we spoke about that painting as we undressed. This is the kind of verbal refuge people like me who can't figure out their feelings retreat to when we are under pressure. Alexa wasn't a big talker but the boy still gave her lots of non-verbal attention, in that equitable way he had about him. By the time we got into bed, I was dizzy with confusion. I ran to the bathroom, vomited, then threw my clothes back on and left.

And here I am, a quarter century later, back in the bathroom hurling, reacting to a triad.

When I'm ready, I summon up as much dignity as I can muster and return to the living room, where we'd been talking. Trevor is gone. I find him in our bed, fully clothed, lying on his stomach. Maybe he's asleep—he likes sleeping face down—or maybe he's faking it. I don't care which it is. I'm glad to have more time to think.

Now that I know about him and Phil, I feel an urgency to take action of some kind. I've always been like that. It doesn't matter how I feel; I must have order. When I found out my parents were divorcing, I was eleven. I wrote out the visitation schedule I wanted for my father, sat the two of them down at the kitchen table, and got them to agree to the terms I had set out.

When Trevor gets up from his nap, I make him a light lunch of lentil soup, sardines on Ryvita, and what's left of the marinated salad I've been living on over the past four days while he was away, supposedly on business. The broccoli, grape tomatoes, and yellow bell peppers perk up the appearance of the plate and he comments on that. Trevor has always been sensitive to the visual aesthetics of a meal.

I don't understand why I'm indulging him. He could have made his own lunch. On the other hand, he hasn't asked me to take care of him like this. I'm just following my routine.

Was it wrong of me to laugh once I'd cornered him

into confessing? It was a nervous reaction. How can I let him stay? Surely I don't need to keep cooking colourful meals for him forever, just to atone for a nervous reaction?

"Hey," Trevor says, "you're a million miles away. Please, come back."

It's true, I have a habit of ignoring his presence when I'm trying to sort out our problems. It's hard to come up with rational solutions and simultaneously try to deal with events in real time.

His cowlick is sticking up. Whenever he has just gotten out of bed he has a boyish cowlick on his crown. It takes effort and gel for him to tame it down. Oh no. Another unwanted image, this time a moving picture. Phil Sterling is placing the sausagelike thumb and index finger of his right hand on Trevor's crown. He gathers up the cowlick, runs his thumb and finger up the length of the cowlick. Removes his hand, places his ugly, cracked lips on the crown and kisses it.

I am taken by nausea again, run to the bathroom and this time I convulse with huge dry heaves. I have not experienced anything like this since the early weeks of my only pregnancy. Three months of misery and then I lost the baby anyway. I am a forty-four-year-old artist, not an expectant mother, not a bulimic teen. This must stop.

But Trevor has always been persuasive, and he talks me into trying it his way. I believe he wants me to be an enlightened person who understands that he loves and cherishes me, and who accepts his freedom to explore the other side of his sexuality.

I find my own attitude interesting. I object only to the betrayal, not to Trevor's lover being male, or to the specific person he has chosen. I don't think I would see the situation any differently if the lover were a woman.

At least they're using protection. Of course they are protecting each other from disease that way. But could it also be an act of goodwill toward the wives?

* * *

Thursday evening. Trevor will be here in fifteen minutes. I have set strict rules. Visiting hours are seven o'clock to eight forty-five. No alcohol or dinner, no talking about anything I don't want to discuss. I'm so determined to keep a lid on the situation that we aren't getting anywhere. It's all been impersonal talk about books and movies. That's fine with Trevor. He knows exactly where he stands. He'll move back home in a heartbeat, if I will only let him.

At first, we did it his way, continued living together. He seemed comfortable, but for me, the situation was so awkward and I threw up so often that after two weeks, I realized he had to leave. I have things to figure out now, and to do that I need some distance from him. I made only one concession to him, by agreeing to hold our highly regulated weekly get-togethers at the house rather than in a coffee shop. Since his move-out, I've kept my food down.

He shows up with a bottle of red wine. Casillero del Diablo, my favourite. Bastard.

"You know the rules," I say.

"Hope springs eternal," he says, sounding feminine. I don't remember hearing that girliness in his voice before. Has it always been there? Or has he been watching those television programs full of flamboyant gay men fixing up the wardrobes, apartments, and relationships of their straight friends?

But our session tonight is more serious than usual. Once he has gotten past his glamorous entrance, Trevor settles back into the most thoughtful version of himself. He curls up into his overstuffed chair and goes quiet. In this spot he has always reminded me of a little boy. In fact I think the man-boy quality that sometimes surfaces is part of what attracted me to him thirteen years ago. But I am just starting to understand that.

"What's on your mind?" I ask in spite of myself.

"Paula's worse. She's back in hospital."

"Her heart again?"

Trevor nods. He tells me he never visits her; all his information comes from Phil. But still, Trevor says, he worries a lot about Paula.

"Why? You hardly know her."

"I don't know why."

"It's guilt."

"Maybe it's compassion."

"I doubt it. Does she know about you guys yet?"

"Never. Phil wouldn't do that to her."

"Do *what*? He's already messing her over by cheating. Why doesn't he come clean and let her get on with her life?"

"Gwen, honey," he says, "you don't understand. Paula is fragile. We need to shield her."

This remark sickens me into utter silence. For the rest of the visit, Trevor rambles on about how he is decorating his new apartment. Now I'm sure he's been watching those TV shows.

After he leaves, I go to the kitchen for a corkscrew and a glass. Then I settle in with the Casillero del Diablo.

* * *

I've never bought the concept that all women are my sisters, nor am I one to seek out people I don't know well, so it's not clear to me why I am driving to the hospital to visit Paula Sterling. Will I tell her? What good would it do her to know what's going on? In any case, I'm a little hung over after consuming three glasses of that red wine fast and on an empty stomach last night. Maybe my judgment is not at its best.

I go to the admissions desk, ask for her room number. In the elevator up I am still in doubt about why I am going through this exercise. When I get to my destination I see two names on the signs next to door 661: A-Mead, and B-Sterling. I knock lightly, walk in. A white cotton curtain acts as a separator. The patient I see is not Paula.

I tiptoe past Patient Mead's bed. I'm not sure why I'm moving with such caution. She's not asleep; she's sitting up in bed. In fact, she gestures to me to come closer. I go and stand by her bedside. She is eighty, maybe more, skinny and pale.

"L-X-G-T-S-B," Mead says. "R-M-J-D. Or put it another way, T-P-Q-J-F."

She articulates the letters with great care. I wonder whether she might have been a radio announcer in better days. She has enormous, almost blindingly white teeth. I wonder why her family has not bought her natural-looking dentures. Would they have cost that much more than these painted horse teeth? Or maybe she has no family.

"W-B-V," she says, distinguishing clearly between the bee and the vee. "H-F-K-C-N."

"Thank you for sharing that with me, Ms. Mead," I say. I just stand there for a few seconds, wondering why she chooses only consonants, and why I am here. Then I force myself to get on with my mission.

"Paula?" I half-speak, half-call.

"Guilty," she says. "Please come in. Just step around the curtain."

She seems surprisingly okay. I assumed she'd look as if she were at death's door. Mind you, I'm unaccustomed to visiting people in hospital and don't have too many points of comparison. Paula is in her mid-sixties, I'd say, and on the stocky side—not even close to Phil's size, but still, large. Her hair is dyed an auburn that works perfectly with her skin tone. She is wearing subtle daytime makeup, skilfully applied. If she weren't sitting up in a hospital bed and hooked up to an IV, I wouldn't know she was sick. That puts me on edge.

"Gwen," she says. "Lovely to see you."

She doesn't seem surprised I'm here, although we know each other so superficially. I'm even further off balance now.

"Hi, Paula. When do you figure they'll spring you?"

What? How did that come out of my mouth?

"Tomorrow, I hope. If I can just get the lipstick and eyeliner on before the doctors do their morning rounds."

She smiles. Me too, I think.

"What's Phil up to these days?" I ask.

"Well, he's…you know…Phil."

"Oh," I say.

"I don't see that much of him."

"No?"

"Not really. I'm so busy with my charity work. My projects. You do what you have to do."

"Projects. Yes."

Say something intelligent, Gwen. But I can't. Where is my silver tongue?

"Of course you have so much to do too," she says. "I have so much respect for artists like you. Especially the women."

"Don't be too impressed. A lot of the time I'm just goofing off in my studio, pretending to work."

"The painting keeps you busy. Takes up many hours."

"Yeah, it's time consuming, that's for sure."

"That's a good thing," she says. "To be caught up in work."

I become aware of a bunch of get-well cards on her end table. They've been here all along but I haven't noticed them until now. "I'm sorry, I say," I should have brought you something."

"You're here," she says. "That's what matters."

"You know, Paula, you look fabulous for a person who's just had a second heart attack."

"Oh my gosh, who told you that?"

"Um, Trevor."

"I've got a testy gall bladder, Gwen, that's all. There's nothing wrong with my heart."

* * *

At home I relive the visit with Paula. I bring myself back to the bedside and hear the words we spoke. I'm good at rewinding. Other people put energy into experiencing immediate emotion; for me, that energy diverts itself into retention and analysis.

I tear the conversation apart, struggle to remember her every utterance and gesture. Had she been talking in code, like Mead? Or was I just attributing meanings to her words that she had never intended? *"That's a good thing. To be caught up in work."* Why? To escape? To drive away the hurt, as Phil fools around? Or maybe she was just admiring a good work ethic.

And why did Phil lie to Trevor about her health? Or was that just Trevor lying to me?

* * *

Trevor has shown up this Monday night with what he calls "evidence," because, he says, he wants to move back home more than ever. He misses me, he says. He shows me books with garish cover designs and multiple exclamation points; asks me to take a few minutes to look at them now. Fine. I'm a fast reader. Women speak out in this book, the wives of gay or bisexual men. These women tell me they live in contentment with their husbands. One says her guy is great at home, good with the kids, and a home reno whiz, but every once in a while he'll go out on the prowl for other guys. It's tough, but she can deal with it. Another woman consents to her man spending the night with other guys a couple of times a week. She stays home and cries all night but it's worth it, she says, so that she can both keep him, and keep him happy. And then there is the woman who organizes picnics every two weeks for the whole family plus her husband's boyfriend. She doesn't like what's going on, but she wants everything normalized for the sake of the kids. So every second Sunday she makes a pastrami sandwich on rye for the guy who is getting it on with her husband. Light on the mustard, just the way the guy likes it.

"We're finishing up early tonight," I say. "Pick up your books and get out of here."

* * *

A month later, he's got something new for me on his Monday evening visit.

"I've sought spiritual advice," he says.

"But you're an atheist," I say.

"I'm not so sure any more," he says. "I've gotten to thinking. Searching."

"Oh?"

"I can rid myself of the ugly stuff I've been carrying around all these years, and be faithful to you. And that's what I intend to do, if you'll have me back."

Oh, I see what's happening here. There's no way Phil was his first.

"Who dumped who?" I ask.

"What?"

"Obviously you've broken up. Were you the one who called it off, or did Phil give you the boot?"

"Must you always think in terms of rejection? It was mutual."

"Really."

"Ish. Mutual-ish."

Okay, so he got dumped and is between boyfriends. In the past he's always been able to find comfort in living with me. And if telling himself lies will bring him the solace he wants, he's good with that.

"You are who you are," I say. "You can't will yourself to be some other animal. Remember Brokeback Mountain?"

"But my spiritual adviser tells me it *can* be done. With faith and self-discipline, I can change."

"I wonder where you found your spiritual adviser," I say. "Let me guess. Online."

"That doesn't take away from his teachings."

"Not at all. Whether he's standing behind a pulpit or sitting at a keyboard to deliver his message makes no difference. It's the same pile of crap either way."

"Open your heart, Gwen," he says. "I want you. I need you."

After he leaves, I open a bottle of the Spanish red and

let myself go a bit. Trevor, my love. I want him too, but I need him like I need inoperable cancer. What I need is the lover I am about to acquire, an Adonis—blonde like me, six feet tall and mightily built. We are completely in synch and our sex life is phenomenal. While we are out on a lovely walk in perfect spring weather, we bump into Trevor. Hi, how are you doing, I'd like you to meet Adonis. Adonis, Trevor. They talk a little, showing more than mere civility. Not sure I like this. I think I see a spark light between them. Could it be? No, there will be none of that. Adonis is too straight, and as for Trevor, well, Trevor wouldn't dare.

Silent Partner

MITCHELL HAS NODDED OFF. He's got his mother's long lashes, and eyelids so delicate they are almost transparent. His eyes race back and forth under those lids. I think that means he is dreaming. What do you dream about when you've only been out of the womb for four months? The warmth of your mother's full breast? The sweetness of her milk? The ring of your father's laugh? What would a nightmare be about? Being left alone. Filling your pants up and getting cold, then hungry. Crying your lungs out for help.

When Mitchell stirs, I unclasp the baby car seat he is sitting in, gently pull away the straps and lift him into my arms. How can a person be so light? I feel honoured that my customer Renata has asked me to keep an eye on him while she is in the fitting room. Many opportunities for me to grow as a human being occur here at Marjorie's Lingerie. Like this one.

When I was a girl, my mother gave me child-rearing tips. She didn't have an agenda; it was just in her nature to pass on knowledge. When you hold your baby, hold him close, she told me. Which is what I'm doing with Mitchell right now, although he is not mine.

He is pursing his tiny mouth, relaxing it, pursing again. I wonder if he is getting hungry.

"He seems to be thinking about mealtime," I call out to Renata.

"Out in two secs," she answers.

Now there's no doubt. With his hands and lips, Mitchell is searching out my breast. Sorry, little buddy, can't help you out with that. I give him the baby finger of my left hand. It's a poor substitute but he sucks with gusto, making the best of an imperfect situation. I'm afraid I may have done the wrong thing, sticking my finger in his mouth. Germs and all that. Then again, I read in a magazine that it's useful for kids to be exposed to germs when they are babies and toddlers. Otherwise they will get sick more often than their classmates once they reach school age. Something about developing immunities.

Renata emerges from the fitting room and says she is happy with the nursing bra she tried on. We do a trade. I hand her Mitchell and she hands me the bra. In a minute she'll have both.

"Can you use a package of the disposable nipple pads?" I ask. "You slip them right into the cups of the bra and wear them between feedings to absorb leakage."

"Sure," she says, and I ring in the sale for both items.

"I wish my mother were more like you," she says, as she signs the credit card receipt.

Now we are entering dangerous waters. I know Renata's mother, Paula; she has been shopping here at Marjorie's Lingerie for twenty-plus years. Paula is a difficult customer—pushy, petty, sometimes rude. She once picked out a nightie that suited her perfectly and I told her so; her answer was "I don't need your compliments." I don't know why she keeps shopping here and often I wish she wouldn't. It's hard to believe that a sweetheart like Renata is her child. But here's the thing: Renata is about to slag her mother and even though I sympathize with her, I can't show favouritism for one customer over the other. The best thing to do right now is to listen, even harder than I have done before.

"My mother is out of her mind," Renata says. "She interferes in every single thing to do with Mitchell. She hates the name we picked for him. She pushes us to put him on solid food right away. She tells me I don't support his head properly when I pick him up. She insists I switch to a different diaper rash cream. Criticism, criticism, criticism...she pounds me with it."

I do feel for Renata but I need to measure my response. What are the right words? I think of something my own mother would say when she was faced with this kind of scenario. You tell the truth and it is up to your listener if she wants to hear beyond your words.

"I'm sure your mother means well," I say.

"Why can't she be more like you?" Renata asks. "You're so non-judgmental. You've never questioned anything about how I take care of my baby."

"I don't see you and Mitchell often and when I do, we're not together for long. Also, we're not related. It's apples and oranges."

"I guess you're right," she says. I can see she is a little disappointed I didn't jump to her defence. I would have liked to do that, too, but to be loyal to both customers, I can't go beyond a certain point on this topic.

Mitchell bawls. He is not too happy with the way his mother and I have set our priorities over the past few minutes. He's been hungry, but now he is famished. He is letting out long, piercing howls with a tremolo. I've learned the meaning of that vibrating cry from having so many mothers and babies in the store over the years: feed me now.

"Do you think your son might like to dine in one of our fine fitting rooms?" I ask.

"That'd be great," Renata says. "Thank you so much."

While she breast-feeds Mitchell in privacy, I do a bit of dusting. It's a Wednesday morning and nobody else is here at Marjorie's Lingerie, so the moment is right for this chore. There's lots to do. Dust accumulates fast everywhere in Calgary's dry climate, no matter how careful you are about cleaning. As I reach the feather duster up to a shelf top, my mind wanders to the early days of my marriage, thirty-two years ago, when Henry and I discussed whether to start a family. We didn't dwell on it, though. We were having a lot of fun as a couple and we used birth control almost without thinking about it. Nothing fancy, just your basic rubbers. They say some men complain about the feel of condoms. Not Henry. We both had plenty of juice. A sheath of latex was not going to get in our way.

But when I reached thirty-three, I began to get nervous about running out of babymaking time. We had long talks, weighed pros and cons, tried to visualize ourselves in the mom and dad roles. We joked that Henry would be a good explainer and I would be a good entertainer for our children, because he had a logical mind and I knew how to tell a funny story. But looking back, I don't think we were clear in our heads about what we wanted. Our conversations were about how we would carry out our jobs as parents, how our lives would change. Us adjusting to kids, that's what we concentrated on. We never speculated much about the kids themselves or how they might feel living with us. That was the big gap in our thinking, only we never realized it.

We tried, but after a year, I hadn't conceived. I got anxious over the failure. Why wasn't it working? I thought we must be missing something. At various times I suggested we try different positions, different days in my cycle. We even experimented a bit with diet. I had read that prunes and eggs might work, so we went through a stage when we had a lot of omelettes with prune compote for dessert. We got mighty sick of all those eggs and the prunes led to diarrhoea, so we stopped. Henry went along with whatever I wanted and stayed cheerful. I think he just wanted me to be happy again and would do anything within reason to make that happen. I completely lost sight of the reason for what we were doing. For me, the whole project became about getting pregnant, not the happy prospect of bringing up a child.

I started taking B vitamins and drinking eleven cups of chamomile tea every day to try to relax. Once again I found myself living on the toilet.

Meanwhile, my periods kept coming. Every time it happened, I was relieved, and that reaction confused me even more. I started having daily talks with myself about whether the babymaking project made sense. If I wanted so badly to become a mother, why did I secretly celebrate every four weeks when I found blood on my panties? Maybe I was afraid of something—pregnancy or birth or raising a child. Or was I just in denial, and did I really wish failure on the baby project?

Henry was kind and caring, but not much help in working this problem out. He had a lot to say when we talked about fishing or politics or his work in accounting or mine in selling and managing. He was full of suggestions on how not to take stress home from work, how to motivate employees, how to deal with impossibly difficult people. He could talk forever about the joys of poker, the ignorance of his two sisters who hated me, the way to percolate a perfect pot of coffee. But when it came to the babymaking project, Henry just let me drive and, except to calm and reassure me, he pretty well held his tongue. He was the silent partner.

When I turned thirty-five, I sat down with him and said I thought we should stop trying for a while. I was exhausted and mixed up because of all the failure and especially because of my relief at the failure. Henry said fine and we went back to using birth control. I never saw him behave that passively about anything else in our marriage.

We never did go back to trying. The subject of babies versus no babies came up occasionally, but as I moved into my late thirties, the question bothered me less. It was one of those things you don't resolve a hundred percent, but after a while you sense how it's bound to go.

Sometimes I get curious about what would have happened if we had tried again and hit the baby jackpot. After all, I lost Henry only twelve years into the marriage. He was in a terrible car crash and died of his injuries nine long days later. If we had had a child together, maybe that would have brought me some comfort.

It's possible. But maybe that child would have had constant nightmares because of losing his father when he was little. Once he reached school age, he would have felt different and set apart from his classmates because he had suffered a loss they couldn't understand. Then they would start treating him as if he were crazy and that would only add to his loneliness. Besides, where would he have found a male role model? I'd be too affected by grief myself to go new-daddy shopping. Anyway, chasing men has never been part of my nature. I'd have to be both parents to our son, and who knows if I would have been up to the challenge? Probably not. So our boy would be a struggler all his life. What a prospect.

If Henry had lived a normal life span, our son might have been okay. But then in his old age, Henry would get Alzheimer's, which is what had happened to his own father in his last years. Our son helps out with his care but there is nothing we can do to prevent Henry's mental deterioration. Then, long after Henry and I are dead, our son comes down with Alzheimer's. He has the early onset kind and by the time he is fifty-four, he can no longer read or button up his own shirt. Gradually he loses the power of speech. He lives in a special care institution that smells of dying brains. At twilight each day he becomes agitated and paces back and forth in his tiny white room. A dozen times he has wandered off the hospital grounds and been brought back by police. The illness grows worse by the month and yet his heart keeps pointlessly beating. Our son finally does not know that he exists.

That's not a future I would want for any child of mine.

I enjoy being around babies. I do. Not the same way as my friend Doreen Lockhart, who goes gaga every time she is in the presence of anybody less than two years old. She has a baby granddaughter, Madison. We can't go anywhere, Doreen and I, without her needing to make a quick stop at a children's clothing store to pick up a new outfit for Madison. Doreen says she has never gotten over her yearning. Each time she sees an infant or toddler, she wants another of her own. Here she is, over sixty, wanting to face another pregnancy. The feeling soon passes but while she's got it, it's real.

Renata and Mitchell come out of the fitting room. Mitchell's head is lolling and his eyes are half open. He looks like a perfectly content drunk.

"Can I give him one more hug before you go?" I ask.

"Of course," Renata says.

He feels soft and beautiful in my arms.

Au Lait Ole

I WISH THE KIDS would get on with their business. The sooner they puke, the sooner we can get out of here.

It's not our first trip to Emergency at the children's hospital. It was my fault the first time, when Danny fell on his head. And it's my fault this time too. I should have just told Laura, No, I won't be able to drop him off to play with Ira for the afternoon. Laura is even more disorganized with Ira than I am with Danny. I should have known something would go wrong. Then, when I get here, I see my kid in that oversized hospital gown and I start laughing like a happy drunk. What kind of a mother reacts like that?

Now Danny and Ira and I are playing in the examining room with the striped rubber ball I threw into my purse as I ran out of the house. The boys are going for the ball, giggling, doing everything but throwing up, which is the one thing we need them to do. They have their stainless steel kidney bowls and their marching orders. But they're two years old; how can they possibly understand the importance of getting that stuff out of their system?

Danny has never excelled at doing what other people

want. When he was born, everyone told me to breastfeed. But Danny refused to latch on. Who could blame him? I wasn't keen on it myself. I figured that if a guy was going to hang off my breast, it ought to be someone closer to my age. The head nurse came in to straighten us out. I could tell that she had been taking care of newborns and mothers for too long. She looked babyworn.

"Listen, my dear," she said, "you made this boy, and you can make him suck."

Made him? Who died and made me God?

Laura has gone back to the waiting area now. She has called her boyfriend Hieu and he is rushing down to meet her there. I was the one who set up Laura and Hieu five months ago. It's not The Great Love, but he's reliable and considerate, and God knows, Laura deserves a break. Her ex took off on her while she was giving birth to Ira. It came out that he had been seeing another woman all the way through Laura's pregnancy. We picked a couple of winners to get knocked up by, Laura and me.

What'll happen if these kids don't vomit soon? Stomach pumping? Dialysis? How much danger are they in? How long will it take?

A young nurse looks in and flashes an unbearably perky smile. "Anything yet?" she chirps.

"Anything yet?" That's all I heard from Luke once I'd missed a period. We hadn't been going out for long when we had one of the mechanical failures I've become famous for. The first pregnancy test was inconclusive. Ten days later, I peed into the bottle again. Positive. Luke quit the scene faster than you could say Broken Condom. When I was two months pregnant, the lawyers' letters started coming: *Our client unequivocally denies that he is the alleged father of the alleged child you allege to be bearing*. Maybe I should have named the kid Al. Short for Alleged.

Hieu has arrived. He and Laura have joined us in the examining room. I'm reading the boys a picture book called *Magic in the Air*. It's about hot air balloons. I am trying to be responsible.

Once, Luke came close to showing a mote of responsibility. Close but no cigar. Rang my doorbell late one night when I was about three months pregnant. As soon as I stepped onto the front porch, he pulled a hundred dollar bill out of his pocket and tried to hand it to me. I folded my arms.

"What's this, a down payment?" I asked.

"Sort of," he said. "There's still time to get rid of it."

For the dozenth time, I told him I had already had my lifetime dose of abortions. He shoved the money at me anyway. A hundred bucks. That should meet Danny's needs nicely to age eighteen.

Hieu has an idea. Let's order pizza, he says, while we wait for the boys to respond to the syrup of ipecac the doctor has given them. *Respond*. What a genteel word to describe hurling. Laura and Hieu and I talk pizza. We settle on size and toppings and which pizzeria to call. One large all-dressed please, to the kids' hospital emergency ward. Hold the anchovies. Should be good for a laugh.

Danny and I always find stuff to laugh about, even when there's really nothing. Our favourite place for laughing is Café Au Lait Ole, two blocks west of our apartment building. The café is full of little kids and mothers. Carol, the hands-on owner, has set everything up to make us comfortable. For the toddlers, state-of-the-art high chairs with padded seats. Carpeted play area. Beginner puzzles, stuffed animals, cardboard picture books. Huge women's washroom with two changing tables.

Every day at the end of my shift, I pick up Danny at day care. We hop on the bus and get off in front of Au Lait Ole. When I walk in there, I don't feel like a struggling single parent doing hard time as a supermarket cashier. I feel that I'm a part of something—a respected member of the Au Lait Ole community. Carol knows all of us by name. The kids are drawn to her like moths to a light. Danny hangs out in the play area and makes new friends. As for the moms, we schmooze. People openly breastfeed their kids while sipping decaf cappuccino. Au Lait Ole is where Danny and I first met Ira and Laura.

Laura is paying as much attention to Hieu as she is to her kid. That's okay; I'm glad things are working out for them. Why else would I have fixed them up? Myself, I've gone celibate. It's been a couple of months now. I'm going to hold out as long as I can. My problem is, I crave the cuddling. If only men would settle for cuddling. Not that I'm anti-sex, but let's face it, you're only as safe as the technology. Three broken condoms; three pregnancies. Is that really my fault? The pill was a bust too—out-of-control weight gain; crippling depression.

Hieu has gone out into the waiting area again, to make sure we don't miss the pizza delivery. Laura and I are trying to keep the little boys entertained. The examining room seems to shrink as the boys grow more restless. Laura is reading them a storybook about a wolverine family. Ira leaps up and runs around in small circles like a bee in a death dance. Now Danny is up doing jumping jacks. Nobody is listening to Laura except me, and I don't care that much about the wolverines. How many pills could those kids have swallowed, and still have this much energy?

The perky nurse looks in. "Any luck?" she asks.

Luck. There's a concept. How did luck factor in that morning when Danny was three months old? He lay on the changing table, and in the nanosecond it took me to reach for a fresh diaper, he rolled over and fell. I heard his head clunk on the hardwood floor and thought I had disabled him for life. But all the way to the hospital, he laughed. Of course, they checked him out for concussion and I don't know what else. Brain damage? Spinal cord injury? Whatever problems they looked for, he didn't have them. He was fine.

And now? Will he be fine this time? What if he winds up with a permanently damaged liver? One distracted single mother leaves her kid in the temporary care of another, and what do you get? Two little boys with liver disease.

The doctor comes in and talks to us. I feel good about this emergency ward doctor. She's got lots of energy and a sense of humour. Hasn't been wrecked by too many years in an institution yet. She says she doesn't want to do anything extreme at this point, especially since we don't know how many pills they swallowed. Maybe a lot, maybe none. She thinks the ipecac will work; it's just a matter of time.

"Okay, men," she says. "Let's see if we can achieve critical mass here." She gives each of the boys another spoonful.

Within a couple of minutes, Ira starts gagging. Then Danny. Now both boys are throwing up into the kidney bowls. While they are heaving, Hieu comes to the door of the examining room and announces that the pizza has arrived. That's one thing Hieu needs to work on—timing.

Laura called earlier this afternoon and told me what had happened. She had been cleaning the living room and she left the boys in her bedroom. Ira hated the sound of the vacuum cleaner, so Laura closed the bedroom door. When she went back to check on them later, they had gotten into a bottle of coated aspirin. Peach-coloured pills were scattered all over the bedspread, and the boys had some in their hands. Ira had a pill in his mouth; she was able to get him to spit it out. She had no clue how many they had swallowed. We arranged to meet here at Emergency. On the way over, I kept asking myself, Why wasn't I spending a Saturday afternoon with Danny anyway? Why did I leave him at Laura's? What was I thinking? What would happen to Danny and Ira? That's the worst part. The suspense. The not knowing.

The boys have finished doing their thing. We clean them up and get ourselves organized. The medical people give us the okay to go. I tell Hieu and Laura that I'm beat; I'm going to have to pass on the pizza. I try to give Hieu my share of the price anyway; I think it's only fair. He waves the money away; tells me not to worry about it.

Danny and I know what we need right now. Refuge.

At Au Lait Ole, Carol gives us her big hello and gets her hug from Danny. She tells me she is looking for feedback from customers. Mother's Day is coming up and she wants to offer something fun and different. I suggest that she run a special on decaf breast milk lattes. Then I tell her about the excitement Danny and I have been through today. Why did it take so long for Danny to vomit, I wonder?

"It wouldn't have," Carol says, "if you had stuck your finger down his throat."

Dartboard

HAROLD WAVERLING, STICK MAN creep. He didn't talk, just aimed. I couldn't see what he was holding in the clenched hand above his head. He was too far away, on the top of the four step wood staircase leading up to our triplex. I was at the far end of our front sidewalk. I covered my fear.

"Put it down, Harold. You don't wanna do it. Just put it down."

He lowered the arm slowly.

"That's it."

Now he dropped whatever he was holding, so I knew I was safe. I relaxed, continued on my way up the walkway.

He reached down fast, picked the thing up, swung. I felt the blow to my forehead. Dead centre. I inhaled hard, could not release. Couldn't breathe as I ran up the sidewalk, took the outside stairs in two steps, pushed open the heavy oak door, shoulder first, and ran up the two flights of indoor stairs. When I got to the landing of our flat, the air whooshed out and I cried in heaves, until the first shock subsided.

I got a clean washcloth out of the linen closet, ran cold water over it and wrung it out. Put it on my head and tilted back slightly so that I could move around without it sliding off. I was experiencing pretty good pain, as my mother would have put it. He had a nerve, that kid. He was ten, just a year younger than me, but he looked eight. Was that his problem? With his cantaloupe-shaped oversized head and skinny frame, he did look like a living stick man. Maybe he had seeds for brains.

Why did he hate me? I hadn't done a thing to him, just said hello a few days back, when my mother had invited me to head down to the second floor landing with her, knock on the door and greet the new family. The Waverlings had only been living in the building since May first, moving day in Montreal. They were on the middle floor, between the Ouellettes and us. I didn't care to be part of my mother's personal welcome wagon, but she kept saying it would be good for me to listen to Eleanor Roosevelt's advice to do one thing that scared me every day. Besides, she said, she would have more courage in my company. She waited, then asked me again, and although I was still not sold on the idea, I gave in. While I stood awkwardly by her side with a bowlful of her gingerbread men, she knocked at their door. She and Mrs. Waverling introduced each other and Mrs. Waverling accepted the cookies with thanks.

"They're even wearing ribbons," she said.

"Without his bow tie, a gingerbread man feels naked," my mother said.

Mrs. Waverling smiled, then said she'd like us to meet the rest of the family. Claire wasn't home, but Harold was, so she made him get out of his room and come to say hello. He made a one-second appearance, grabbed one of the cookies and disappeared. You could tell he was annoyed. But was that a reason to hurt me later? It wasn't as if that visit had been my idea.

In a way Harold was like Henry in the comic books. They didn't talk much—well, Henry didn't talk at all—and they both had melonheads. But Henry wouldn't hurt an aphid, whereas Harold pinned ants to the front lawn of our building and burned them to death in the sun under a magnifying glass.

Now my head and pride were hurt and I wanted to hear my mother's voice. We had gotten much closer since my father's passing three years earlier. Leaping leukemia, the doctors called his cancer. I adored him and took the death hard. My mother let me talk about it whenever I wanted, but she never said much about her own reaction to losing him. I didn't think then about what she might be feeling. That kind of wondering was left for my adult years.

I called her at work. First she asked practical questions. Was I dizzy? Throwing up? Seeing double?

"Good—no scary symptoms," she said. "Sounds like you got a nasty whack, but you'll be all right."

"I want Harold to get into trouble," I said.

"I'll give Rita Waverling a call when I get home. She needs to know what her boy is up to anyway."

I poured myself a glass of milk, got some Oreos. I moved to the living room and tried to get myself comfortable, ignore my headache, forget how I wanted Harold dead. I would distract myself with television. My mother had won our first ever set the year before. Since then, the TV and I had become pretty good friends.

Now my favourite cartoon was on—*Rocky and His Friends.* Today Rocky the Flying Squirrel and Bullwinkle Moose were transporting Mount Flatten, which could float because it was full of natural deposits of the antigravity metal upsidaisium, so it was up to Rocky and Bullwinkle to save their country. Bullwinkle's uncle had left him the mountain in his will and the United States government desperately needed upsidaisium. There were puns and pranks galore, which usually cracked me up, but not today. What did I care about those wild animals and their mission anyway? I lived in Canada.

I turned the TV off and stewed in silence over the wrong Harold had done me. I checked the time. Five o'clock. My mother would just be getting off work. She'd wait for the bus and then travel through the rush hour. It usually took her an hour to get home. She was skilled at dealing with people; I didn't trust myself in that department. She would know what to say to Mrs. Waverling. I had to be patient.

But the pressure built up inside me until I had to act.

I headed down to the second floor.

A teenager came to the door. This must be Claire. She was fine-featured and slender and wore her honey blonde hair in a page boy. Like me, she hadn't yet changed out of her school uniform. But she wore the elegant high school tunic—a form fitting v-neck. And more importantly, it was belted with a non-regulation black tasselled sash. The sash had only recently come into fashion and, at least in our district, Outremont, teachers were turning a blind eye to it. They must have realized that even a dress code can't defeat a powerful trend.

Claire wore the sash like it was custom made for her. I felt inferior in my square-necked elementary school tunic with the regulation self-belt secured by two plain buttons. Claire looked me over and I lost any leftover confidence. Then I lost the power of speech.

She waited, finally spoke.

"Yeah?"

"Can I please speak to your mother?" My voice came out a little louder than I wanted.

"She's at work."

Of course. I should have realized. My mother had told me that Mrs. Waverling had a job at the post office.

Now what should I say? I had no plan, just a burning need for justice.

"You're Claire, right?"

"Yeah. Look, do you need something?"

"I'm Irene from upstairs."

"I know."

"Your brother threw a rock into my head."

"Into it? There's a rock inside your head?

"*At* it."

"Oh. Yeah, I see the bump now."

"So."

"So?"

"Tell your mother, okay?"

"Why? I didn't see it happen."

She closed the door.

I ran back upstairs and sat down again my brooding position—elbows on kitchen table, hands clenched, eyes staring straight ahead.

* * *

When my mother got home, she took care of first things first. Sympathy. A kiss on the head bump to start the healing. Questions about whether I was still all right, not feeling woozy. Cooking. Supper. Dishwashing. Some evenings I dried the dishes, but my mother told me not to bother tonight, just to rest. Once the cleanup was done, she sat down at our telephone table in the alcove. She dialed slowly; that was her way when she had a tricky call to make.

"Hello, Rita?" she said, "It's Patty from upstairs. Have you got a few minutes to chat?...Oh, good. So how are you liking our district so far?"

The conversation went on like that for a few minutes, with talk of how fast the kids were growing and with my mother sympathizing about how tough it is to adjust to new digs, to meet new people, to become familiar with a new neighbourhood. Never changing her warm tone, and in a natural way, she moved into describing what had happened between Harold and me in the afternoon. She didn't make Harold sound like the heller he was; she just gave the facts of the incident, as she understood them from me. Then she listened. After that the call didn't go on for long.

"What's his punishment?" I asked when my mother got off.

"God knows. Maybe she'll spank him with a kleenex."

"What? He uses my head as a dartboard and gets away with it?"

"It looks that way. She made excuses for him. Sounds like she's used to it. I wish she'd punish him when he acts up like that—teach him to control himself. Then there might be hope for the kid."

"What do you care about him? What about me?"

"You'll be fine, Irene," she said. "A bump on the head is temporary."

* * *

After that I was careful to avoid Harold. If he was in the back lane throwing a tennis ball against a building so hard it looked as if he would dent the bricks, I'd go to the front walk to swivel in my hula hoop. If he was on our front lawn tearing legs off insects, I headed off to the back lane for a bouncing session with my bolo bat. I knew he couldn't hurt me for the moment, and I told myself that was good enough. Otherwise, I would have had no peace.

* * *

The next week, Harold got a one-day suspension for beating up a girl in the schoolyard. Everybody knew, because suspensions were so rare at our school. Mrs. Waverling asked the principal, Mr. Macdonald, to let Harold serve the detention in the office, so that she could work her shift at the post office. But Macdonald said no, so she had to leave the brat on his own all day. She knew Harold would leave the flat and wander around the neighbourhood doing whatever he pleased. But, as my mother said, what choice did Mrs. Waverling have?

* * *

I saw Claire a little over a week later, on a Friday afternoon, at Rothstein's Confections. She was standing behind the counter with Sarah Rothstein, who also went to Outremont High. Sarah was in no shape to concentrate on customer service, as she was crying her eyes out. Nobody else was in the store. I had come in to buy a bottle of Nesbitt's Orange, but the bottle opener, the straws and the soft drink cooler were all kept behind the counter. It wasn't as if I could put my money on the counter, grab what I needed and go. I would have to ask for what I wanted and Sarah would have to answer me and then do a couple of things. I didn't want to bother with all that, but I did want the drink. So I left, walked a couple more blocks and bought my Nesbitt's at Perrin Brothers on Ducharme and MacEachern.

After supper, I did a full Haroldcheck and then started a game of hopscotch against myself on the front walk. Within a few minutes Claire came along, heading home. We said hello to each other and this time she seemed neutral toward me, not mad. I thought it might be all right for me to say something more.

"You were nice to Sarah today."

"She needed a friend, that's all."

"Do you know what's bugging her?'

"Yeah, but it's none of your beeswax."

She walked on and I threw one of my playing stones to number seven on the sidewalk, then hopped over to the number seven segment, picked up the stone and came back, all the while thinking about Claire and the things she had and hadn't said. I liked that she hadn't blabbed. It was the second good thing I had seen her do today. If I had a problem and told someone about it, I wouldn't want the whole city hearing about it either. Sarah had chosen the right person to confide in and I was ashamed that I had probed.

I suspected that Sarah was pregnant. Not long after my father died, a new column had started up in the Montreal Star, which my mother would bring home every night. My mother loved this column and she would often read it out loud to me and then we would discuss it. People would write letters to a wise woman about stuff that was bugging them and she would write back to give them advice. This was how I found out that a teenaged girl should not go all the way with her boyfriend or else she would get into trouble and then the boy would disappear. Because of shame, her parents would send her far away to go through the pregnancy and give birth. To anyone who asked, they would say that she was visiting relatives, whether that was true or not, and she would be forced to give the baby up for adoption. She would suffer from loneliness and confusion and lose her good reputation forever. And even before a girl showed, you could tell she was in trouble, because she cried a lot.

* * *

In the weeks that followed I often saw Claire and Sarah after school at Rothstein's Confections. They'd be dusting shelves, straightening out stock, or just sitting behind the counter on stools, not doing anything. Sarah's father was there too, handling the customer service end of things.

Then both of them stopped showing up at the store. I saw Claire in our building and around the district, but there was no sign of Sarah. I got kind of worried that the parents had already sent her away. After a couple of weeks, I got up the nerve to ask Mr. Rothstein where she was. He said she was spending some time with her grandparents in Florida.

"But it's still the school year," I said.

"They've got schools in Miami," he said.

Schools? Did he take me for an idiot? My classmate Shayna Gold had gone to Miami over Christmas vacation and brought back seashells for all of us. For us Montrealers, Miami meant palm trees, beaches, hot weather in December. With his answer, Mr. Rothstein cleared up all my doubts. First I had seen Sarah cry as if her life was done. Now she was thousands of miles away and her father had made up a fairytale reason. Why would he do that, if he wasn't ashamed?

* * *

I was puzzled that Sarah's suffering in pregnancy bothered me so much. I only knew her from Rothstein's Confections. I would ask her for a 7 Up, wax lips, Double Bubble gum; she would take my money, hand me my purchases and count the change out into my palm. That was all we saw of each other.

The few times Claire and I bumped into each other, we said hi and left it at that. One Saturday evening a boy came to pick her up and they walked out of the building hand in hand. I was sitting outside on the steps reading my *Calling All Girls* magazine. She greeted me, but didn't introduce him. That was okay. I didn't know what to say to a teenage boy anyway. I thought how beautiful it was that they were holding hands. I had never done that with a boy, except in my uncontrolled fantasies about Dr. Ben Casey, the TV neurosurgeon.

By Monday I couldn't stand it any more. I had to know that Sarah was okay. I asked my mother for advice.

"Look," she said, "you can't keep eating yourself up about this. The best thing is to talk with Claire again. Just be honest and explain that you're worried about Sarah. Tell her you know how to be discreet."

I decided I'd invite Claire for a walk in Rockland Park. I did like to visit that park. I'd pull petals off wild daisies to find out if Dr. Casey loved me or not. I'd go all the way down to the railroad tracks, watch the CP trains roll by. I'd wave to the engineer, count the box cars, wave to the caboose man. I'd visit the abandoned shuffleboard courts and picture myself in a group of rich people enjoying a Sunday afternoon game many years back. I'd hit a pop fly with an imaginary bat, run all the bases in the baseball diamond, and bring in a home run. Rockland Park was the place where I spent time being nostalgic about good old days that I had never known.

When I got home from school on Tuesday I headed downstairs, knocked on the door. Claire answered. I told her I was off for a walk in the park and invited her along.

"I'm kinda busy," she said. "My English teacher assigned us an essay. 'Hamlet has a fatal flaw. Discuss.'"

She saw my disappointment.

"All right, but just for a half an hour," she said.

We didn't talk much for a while. Then I asked about her boyfriend. She said his name was Scott. He had graduated from the High School of Montreal two years earlier and was working to get his welder's ticket.

"What's a welder's ticket?" I asked.

"It's like a degree. But you need to do something practical to get it, instead of just reading and writing and shooting your mouth off."

We walked in silence for another few minutes.

"I'm worried about Sarah," I said.

"Why? You're not friends, are you?"

"Not really. I just know her from the store."

"So what do you care?"

"I don't know. I just do. I haven't been able figure out why. I've gotta know she's all right. That's all."

"Okay. Do you know how to keep your big trap shut?"

"Yeah."

"She's down in Florida, and not for a holiday. She never wanted to go there in the first place and she writes me once a week and every letter says the same thing. She's miserable. She wants to come home. But it's not time and she can't. Not yet."

"So when will they let her come back?"

"I think she'll have to wait until the bubbie croaks."

"Eh? The baby's gonna croak?"

"The bubbie. That's what Jewish kids call their grandmothers. You live in Outremont and you've never heard of a bubbie?"

"But what about the baby?"

"What baby? What are you talking about?"

"Nothing. Never mind."

"Wait a minute. You mean you thought…I don't believe it. Have you lost your marbles?"

"Um…"

"You've got some nerve. Sarah's not that kind of girl. She hardly even dates."

"I'm really sorry."

"Who did you blab to?"

"Nobody."

"Baloney. Who?"

"Just my mother."

"Jesus."

"She won't say anything. She knows how to be discreet."

"She better."

"But I don't get why Sarah's down there now, before summer vacation starts."

"Because, dummy, dying people don't always fit in with the school calendar."

* * *

"NOT THIS TIME, MOM. NO."

I had never heard Claire lose control before. My mother and I got bits of what she was saying, but she was bawling and also screaming, so a lot of words came out blurred or half formed. We could hear Mrs. Waverling's voice, but it wasn't loud enough for us to make out what she was saying.

How could we figure out what had happened? On our block, we were all jammed close together and doors and windows were left open in spring and summer. Everybody knew just enough about everybody else's business to get it wrong.

A door slammed. Then, nothing.

"Families," my mother said, and shook her head. "Now let me have another look at that bruise."

We went into the bathroom and I lifted my shirt. My mother stood behind me, gently patted the middle of my back. "Healing," she said.

The day before, I'd been sitting on the front walk sorting my marble collection, when I felt something pound into my back. It was Harold Waverling's booted foot. I'd been lucky since the rock-in-head incident. We'd had a couple of skirmishes but he hadn't hurt me much. But I had always been afraid that he'd catch up with me eventually, give me something else to remember him by. Harold, the stick man melonhead with feet so light you couldn't hear him coming. My mother was worried enough that she took me to Dr. Shatsky to get my back checked out. Just bruising, he said. No damage to the spinal cord.

Once again my mother talked to Mrs. Waverling, who dug into her mental excuse jar and pulled out another lame one. The day of the kick, he'd been sick with a head cold, she said. All stuffed up, and not thinking straight.

So he wouldn't have kicked me on a day when his sinuses were clear?

"Boy," my mother said, "Rita Waverling should become a defence lawyer or something. She's a regular Perry Mason."

The next evening Mrs. Waverling called my mother and asked if she would please send me down to talk to Claire, who hadn't left her room except for trips to the washroom and to grab the odd drink of water. She wouldn't talk to her mother at all.

"What do you say?" my mother asked.

"Okay, but only if Harold isn't there."

"Don't be silly. He's not going to go after you with his mother around. Harold is hotheaded, not stupid."

* * *

"Claire?"

Nothing.

"It's me. Irene. Can I come in?"

No answer.

"You okay?"

I sat there for a couple of minutes, biting off the cuticles on my right hand while holding a record, a 45, in my left.

"Claire. I'm not gonna sleep tonight if we don't talk. I'm a nervous wreck."

She opened the door.

"Hey," I said, "You wanna listen to this with me? It's Connie Francis." She loved Connie Francis the way I loved Dr. Ben Casey, only without the lust.

She clipped a red plastic adapter into the centre of the record, got her record player going, and within a few seconds Connie was with us, half-sobbing and half-belting "Who's Sorry Now?" She didn't bother with the B-side, just played "Who's Sorry Now?" twice more. Her mother knocked on the door and this time, Claire let her in. Mrs. Waverling offered us food but Claire asked for snack money instead, and her mother was so relieved to get her daughter back, she agreed. Claire and I walked over to Bingman's Deli on Dollard, across the street from the Stern's supermarket. We each had a coke, a smoked meat on rye, pencil-thin french fries that we speared with toothpicks, and a dill pickle sliced lengthwise down the middle. Claire was so hungry she didn't chew carefully enough, and got a stomach ache on the way back.

We didn't talk much until we had passed Lowery's Electric, halfway home. Claire began to cry and spill at the same time, kind of like she had done with her mother the day before, only this time she wasn't as loud, and also we were side by side, so I could make out what she was saying.

"I'm sick of doing my mother's dirty work," she said.

"Like what?" I asked.

"Harold is a putz, and she won't punish him, and I'm supposed to be the guard dog, keeping away all the people he's injured."

"What's a putz?" I asked.

"Eh? Do you live in Outremont or don't you?"

"Yeah. So?"

"So you're surrounded by thousands of Jewish people. I practically just got here and I already know the most important Yiddish words."

"So what's a putz?"

"A miserable little brat bastard of a prick," she says.

"Wow. That's good."

"Why do you think I'm picking up the lingo? They've got a ton of good ones to help you save your breath. Schmuck. Schlemiel. Schnorer."

"Putz?"

"Attagirl."

"Okay, so who did Harold injure? Besides me, I mean?"

"Where do I start? He snuck up behind Rifka Schwartz and pulled her braids so hard her neck almost snapped. He tripped Sophie Ouellette, made her fall on her face and hurt her nose. And Andrea Borenstein—that one was really bad..."

"Hmm. All girls."

"I think he stays away from the boys because he's afraid they'll beat him up. Us girls, we're taught to be polite."

"Boys are also taught. I know polite boys."

"Me too. Some. Well, maybe he's going after the boys too, and they're not telling. All I know is, my mother makes me deal with the phone calls or answer the door when a girl's parent shows up, and I'm supposed to say things like 'What are you talking about? Did you see him do it? *I* didn't see him do it.' And the idea is, some of them will go away."

"My mother didn't."

"She sure didn't. But a lot do, thanks to Claire the bull-dog."

"Madame Ouellette says bulldogs are too friendly to be guards. She tells all the kids on the street not to be scared of their bulldog Alphonse."

"Fine. Pick your breed. I'm just sick of protecting my mother and my putz of a brother."

"It's not fair."

"No kidding. And then with the parents Mom does have to talk to, like for example your mother, she makes up these crazy health stories. 'Oh, my Harold kicked your daughter, missus? Well, it was an accident. See, he's got an inner ear infection, and it makes him walk like a drunkard, so every once in a while his feet accidentally bump into things. Things like your kid's spleen.'"

"What's a spleen?"

"Jeez, Irene, what do you think I am, a dictionary?"

* * *

My mother and Mrs. Waverling were having a clothesline conversation. The clotheslines were in the back, on the fire escape side of the building, next to the kitchens. It was Sunday, laundry day for some of the women on our street—the ones like Mrs. Waverling and my mother who had jobs outside the home. My mother kept the basketful of clean laundry on her right and a bowl of wooden clothes pins on a folding chair in front of her. She had to lean over to reach the clothesline, which didn't bother her, but I always worried that she would fall three floors down, land on her head, and die instantly. Then I would need to make my way through life with no parents, like Little Orphan Annie in the funnies.

I often criticized her for her loud voice, although I had also inherited it. But sometimes that voice came in handy. Now I could hear every word of her end of the conversation from my place at the kitchen table, where I was sitting to do my homework. Claire's name kept coming up today, so I stepped onto the back balcony. I stood just outside our door, so that Mrs. Waverling wouldn't be able to see me from the floor below. I knew that what I was doing was not exactly right, but this was about Claire, who was sort of becoming my friend. I needed to know.

The gist of it was that Claire told Mrs. Waverling she had split up with Scott, and Mrs. Waverling wasn't pleased. She felt that Claire could have enjoyed a good future with this boy, a stable person with a trade. He was nice to Claire and also to Mrs. Waverling and why should Claire give up such an opportunity? And what did my mother think? My mother said that in her opinion,

Claire should do whatever made her happy. My mother had seen me on the balcony, but she wasn't angry. In fact, on the way back to the kitchen, she rolled her eyes at me, like we were in a conspiracy together.

"You really don't like Mrs. Waverling, do you?" I asked, once the door was safely closed.

"Why do you say that?"

"Just the way you took Claire's side."

"The girl has a right to find her own way. And besides, she's only sixteen. It's a little early for the mother to be angling to marry her off."

In bed that night I thought about how Mrs. Waverling and my mother were both raising kids on their own and should be friends, but never would be, and how Claire and I were five years apart and shouldn't be were friends, but we were.

I knew I had to go for a walk with Claire soon, to give her a chance to spill, before she fell into another funk. I had a mother I could confide in. Claire didn't.

* * *

We were following a different route today, on a major walk that would take us much longer than usual, along Ducharme to Dollard, then up to Van Horne to Bernard, and along Park Avenue all the way to the base of Mount Royal. My mother gave me tickets for the bus home and a couple of dollars for a snack. We'd pick up the 80 by Fletcher's Field, then switch to the 161, get off at Rockland, and walk the remaining couple of blocks to home. There was lots of time to talk.

"Why didn't you tell me you broke up with Scott?" I asked.

"To be honest, I thought you were too young to understand," Claire said.

Maybe I was, but with Sarah away, who could she talk to? I still wanted to help her out, even though I knew I wasn't her first choice.

"So what happened?"

"Oh, you'll find out when you start dating, it doesn't work if the boy likes you more than you like him."

"How can you tell who likes who more?"

"Well, let's say he kisses you and you don't feel much. That's a sign."

"Did he take it hard?"

"Yeah. I feel sorry for him. He's a nice boy."

"Does he have friends?"

"One or two. He'll get over it, but right now he's hurt ing. What can I do? The vital spark isn't there. You know, he even called and asked me to come back to him."

"What did you say?"

" 'You're a swell guy and you deserve someone who loves you.' Stuff like that."

"That sounds nice."

"Tell that to Mom. She thinks I'm the wicked witch of the east."

"I know. She was telling my mother in a clothesline chat yesterday."

"Oh, so that's how you found out."

"Mm-hmm."

"I wish she wouldn't babble about me in public."

"Yeah."

"Your mother doesn't do that to you, eh?"

"No, but she does talk about other people's kids."

"Now the whole block knows I broke up with my boyfriend."

"Only the ones who do their laundry on Sunday."

* * *

After three more run-ins with Harold, I'd had enough and decided to change my approach. The next time he came after me I was ready. I lined up the heel of my oxford with his bony knee and kicked clean through it.

Syntocenon

THIS MORNING I WOKE up to two men—Alden of course, and also Tom Smith, my witty morning radio man. I need to prod Alden to get out of bed. He is a night hawk by nature. I'm not that much of a morning person either but I am highly motivated to get him going, because only by getting to work on time will he keep his job, and at this point, he is our sole breadwinner. To avert a nervous breakdown I left my job at the consumer bureau and so far I haven't been able to find anything else. I am kind of wondering whether my ex-boss is trashing me to prospective employers when they do their reference checks. But why he would want to keep me out of work, I don't know.

"C'mon, sleeping beauty," I say. "Wakeup time."

Alden opens his eyes, scratches his beard, and rolls over. I pull the top sheet and duvet off the bed in one dramatic swoop that makes me feel like Wonder Woman. Then he gets up, all right.

While he showers I throw on my robe and head into the kitchen to prepare his breakfast and brown bag lunch. Meanwhile, I try to get psyched about my 10:30 job interview. It's for a job as a receptionist and I know they are going to ask why I am setting my sights so low. Same reason I was asked why I wanted to stock shelves at the supermarket. Must everyone with a university education seek employment as an astrophysicist or a brain surgeon; that is my question. Can't a person set his or her sights lower in the world of day jobs, while trying to achieve greater personal depth or enlightenment or whatever? Or, for that matter, why can't a person underachieve without being deemed a failure? If I have a good work ethic and can competently do the job that I am hired to do, shouldn't that be enough?

The truth is, between what I went through at the consumer bureau and my mixed up feelings over what happened at the hospital last week, I don't want anything too challenging in a job right now.

* * *

"You don't want to look at this, do you?" the doctor said, as though stating a fact in question form.

I didn't want to deal with It and I could tell from the tone and wording of his question that he didn't want to deal with It either, or maybe he didn't want to deal with my dealing with It. Whatever his motives were, and whatever drove me, I shook my head no and It was removed from my hospital room.

Earlier in the day I had checked in and they had given me my bed and started an IV laced with a substance called Syntocenon, to bring on the pains and expulsion. This was the next step, five days after the bleeding and rupturing of the membrane and the ultrasound that showed It was dead.

"You could wait and let labour start on its own," Dr. Gomberg had said.

"How long?"

"Hard to say. Could be hours; could be weeks."

"But It's dead. Doesn't the body want to get rid of a foreign object? Why wasn't It get pushed out right away?"

"I don't know. There's a lot of variability in the timing."

I could not bear the idea of being a walking tomb. Also, I felt that I had failed It somehow, and I did not want constant reminding of that until such time as my body should come to its senses and expel It. So the hospital option seemed best. I would spend a few unpleasant hours, then put the experience behind me. Of course Alden would be at my side the whole time. It seemed like a plan.

Labour took its own sweet time coming. Meanwhile I was thinking, *Can't I get anything right?* But once the pains were ready, they moved on with a vengeance. It wasn't long before we moved on to delivery, or whatever that event is called when It is dead. Somehow It got stuck in the canal and Doctor Gomberg had to stick his hand right up there, grab It and yank It out. Hurt like hell.

"I'm sorry, Cara," he said.

That comment helped me with the pain. Say what you like, I've got lots of empirical evidence that kindness affects pain. I can tell if a doctor is faking it. That's worse than neutrality. But Gomberg is the genuine article.

After that, the nurse checked up on me often. I felt weak and disoriented; I figured that was normal. But a while later, the doc came back.

"Your bad luck is continuing," he said. "You've got a fever and the placenta hasn't come out. I'll have to do a D and C."

"Will I be awake?"

"No, Cara, you've been through enough. No, you'll go under a general anaesthetic."

"Isn't that risky? Could I die?"

"That's unlikely."

"Then it's possible."

"If I gave you a guarantee, I'd be a charlatan. I'm pretty confident you'll be okay, but there's really only one individual who knows with certainty."

"Who's that?'

He pointed upward. I lost faith five years ago and took no comfort in that gesture.

We got through it, and when we arrived home the next day, Alden took me into his arms.

"You're a good person," he said. "You did your best."

Did I? How could he know? How was doing one's best defined in this situation? If I had truly done my best, wouldn't I have looked?

I am supposed to be in getting-on-with-it mode, but I am nowhere near that point.

* * *

I turn on the TV for distraction and they are running

an ad for Pampers. The baby is sickeningly cute. I press the off switch with more force than necessary. Marilyn Perkins from the consumer bureau sends me an exquisite black orchid that depresses the hell out of me. Cathy Aaronian leaves home-made cookies and a note but does not ring the doorbell. Through the kitchen window I can see her running to her car, quitting the scene to avoid contact, as though I were carrying the Ebola virus.

When Alden gets home from work, I ask if he has any theories about why Cathy ran. "My feeling is that it's fear," he says.

"Of what? I'm not exactly an intimidating person."

"She's afraid it'll happen to her."

"I never knew miscarriage was contagious."

"She's scared to get too close to the experience."

This is one of the things that drew me to Alden in the first place. He has such astute insights into human behaviour.

Later, in bed, he nods off in his usual five minutes. I lie awake for a long time, ruminating. If Cathy is afraid to come near me, who am I to find fault with her? Maybe fear was driving me when I decided not to look at It. What was I afraid of? The way It looked after seventeen weeks' gestation? Or was I just not brave enough to hold It to my heart, because although It was mine, It was also dead?

The next day Cathy phones me. I thank her for the cookies and she offers condolences that sound heartfelt. I realize it was wrong of me to even think of judging her harshly for her decision not to ring the doorbell and come in for a visit yesterday. If I were still a person of faith, I would say I had been sinful in harbouring unkind notions about her. It's a good thing that I have turned my back on religion and can just feel like a shit for my fuck-ups, without also worrying about divine retribution.

I got off the phone and started thinking about Its progress after I refused to look.

Where did they take It? To the morgue? And then where? The garbage? If not, how did they dispose of It? Before they got rid of It, did they preserve some of Its tissue to do further study of—I don't know—the phenomenon of miscarriage? I like the idea that It might have made a contribution to scientific research. I am a great believer in science. Makes a lot more sense than mumbo jumbo religion.

Two weeks later, Dr. Gomberg calls with the results of the amniocentesis that was done a couple of days before the bleeding started. This was the result: It was badly damaged genetically, with a condition that would have left It severely handicapped mentally and physically. Had It been born, It would have lived a maximum of two years and It would have had close to zero quality of life.

"I imagine you have mixed feelings," he said.

Who knows? Right now, I'm numb.

"Do you have any questions?" he asks.

"Just one. What was the sex?"

"Female."

When I am off the phone I have my first good cry

since all the trouble started. Alden holds me close. Later in the evening, we crack open a new bottle of Hungarian red. We lift our classes.

"To Her," I say.

Salk and Sabin

WHEN THE PHONE RINGS I'm at home, it's nine o'clock and I am at the height of what my best friend Doreen Lockhart calls "a worry event." Tonight the star of the show is the H1N1 flu. First of all I don't know how a pandemic is different from an epidemic, which is the word they used when I was a little girl growing up in the fifties and polio was putting kids into iron lungs or leg braces or killing them, until Jonas Salk put on his thinking cap and came up with that dead virus vaccine of his and even tested it on his own family to show he meant business, and then we all lined up for shots and were spared. Thank you Doctor Salk. So is this swine flu thing worth more, less, or the same amount of worry as if the problem were polio? For an Olympic-level worrier like me it is important to know how much nerve-juice to pour into any one problem. Otherwise, I may run out, and what then? Also, if I've got the bug, I don't want to go to work and pass it on to my customers at Marjorie's Lingerie. And I return to my original question—do I have symptoms or not? The stiffness in my lower back that I became aware of an hour ago...I wonder if that counts as muscle pain. Could it be that I am coming down with it, but have such a mild case I don't know it, and have been accidentally transmitting it to unsuspecting underwear purchasers? My customer Barbara Sawchuk's daughter Tracey came down with swine flu at the very end of her pregnancy and developed breathing problems and had to be put on a ventilator; Barbara tells me that is the modern version of an iron lung. They delivered the baby by Caesarean and he lived but Tracey may or may not make it.

What if a pregnant woman walks into Marjorie's Lingerie and I give her swine flu because, for example, I have not washed my hands properly. These days I always count to a hundred and twenty after soaping up, and I scrub like there's no tomorrow, but maybe that's not enough. Last night the TV news anchor was talking about this epidemic—excuse me, pandemic—and he said, "So how much should you worry?" but then did not answer his own question or find anyone else who could answer it.

Anyway here I am in the middle of this worrypalooza when, like I said, the phone rings and who should it be but my best friend Doreen.

"Have you seen today's paper?" she asks.

"The Sun or the Herald?"

"The Globe."

"Oh, you know how I feel about that paper. It's more for educated people like you."

"Irene, give yourself some credit. We're talking about a daily rag, not the collected works of Friedrich Hegel."

"Okayokay. So what's in the Globe today?"

"Well, this woman from Chicago has invented a bra that's dual purpose."

"Every bra serves a dual purpose. Left and right."

"All right, this bra is multipurpose."

She explains and when our conversation ends, I call my friend Julie on her cellphone right away.

"Can you meet me at the Bean Wave in half an hour?" I ask.

"I'm hanging there now," she says. "Come on by."

I walk to the Bean Wave as fast as my sixty-two-year-old legs will carry me, so that I can get onto one of the computers. Oh, I know I should stop resisting, go for it, buy my own computer. But I enjoy not having e-mail and Twitter; I feel no need to be plugged into the whole universe every second. If I had to take care of answering and sending messages constantly, when would I work or walk? When would I think? No, I prefer to head over to my favourite little Internet café when the fancy strikes me. It's just on Seventeenth Avenue, an easy walk from my apartment. Who can't use a bit of extra exercise? And Seventeenth Avenue is well-lit even in the evening, so that, as I cross the street, I don't have to worry too hard about being hit by drivers whose night vision is no better than mine.

Julie has her own little laptop, which her mother bought for her last year in a fit of guilt over not being a good parent. But she still works at the Bean Wave part time to help her pay her steep university tuition and she is often here off-hours to socialize. Usually when we get together, that's where.

"Hey, Irene," she says, and I get my usual warm hug from her, which I hope will not to lead to either of us getting sick with the dreaded virus. She is in her early twenties and the way this bug seems to work, if she picks it up, she is more likely than a lot of other people to get super sick, maybe even die.

"Hi, sweetie," I say, but within a second I am sitting down at a computer, in a rush to log in; this is the way I get when the urge comes to me to do research.

It doesn't take long for me to find what I want, and I am able to get much more detail than Doreen had found in that small article in the Globe. A scientist living in Chicago has invented a new kind of brassiere with special features like a filter device and a breathing device attached to each cup. Well, let's say terrorists attack or your house catches on fire or you find yourself in the middle of a toxic cloud, and only a gas mask will save you. You reach under your blouse and unsnap the specially equipped bra, breaking it into two. You quickly snap a cup over your head, securing it with what used to be a bra strap. And there you go, you've got your gas mask on. Then, because you're not the type who panics in an emergency, you calmly hand the other cup to the guy next to you, who sees what you have accomplished and dons his mask too. One bra, two lives saved.

"What's wrong?" Julie asks. "You've got that tortured look."

"Well, it's just, I can't figure out exactly how this bra

mask works; the websites are all a bit different from each other. Some of them talk about two sets of cups and each cup is detachable, which would make for a four-cupped bra. I don't really get that."

"Inner and outer sections, perhaps?" Julie says.

"That must be it. It's bugging me that I don't get it. Why am I so dense? Why isn't it clear to me how this thing works?"

"Maybe it's not you. Maybe the explanations themselves are unclear."

"No, I think I'm just missing it. Design isn't really my strong point. But the inventor does want to bring it to market as soon as she can."

"If I know you, you'll see to it that Marjorie's Lingerie is the first lingerie retailer in Canada to stock it."

"Maybe we ought to try it out. It might come in handy on those windy Calgary days when you feel like you are walking around in a dust storm."

All the way home I am thinking about the bra mask and its usefulness and how maybe it would come in handy right now with this swine flu all around us. How much more comfortable would a person be in an attractive, well-made face garment than in one of those ugly paper, staples, and elastic band contraptions that pass for masks today? In a solid foundation mask, a person in a dire emergency would know that she looked good. And everyone knows that when you are confident about your appearance, you are that much more likely to think clearly, and succeed in doing whatever you must to get yourself out of that bad situation.

By the time I get home I have convinced myself that the answer to containing swine flu is to get bra masks on the market as fast as possible. I go to bed but sleep is out of the question. I am thinking, now that quite a few of our regulars at Marjorie's Lingerie are getting older, they could probably use some CPR and general first aid training. Why couldn't we bring in emergency medical training guys to teach them, and tie in the classes with a bra mask promo? But maybe the classes would become so popular we would have people lining up outside the store to get in and we'd have to set up priority lists like they are doing with the flu vaccine. Of course the bra masks would become wildly popular. Nobody would want to take the classes unless they could also be guaranteed the bra masks. We would become unable to meet the demand as it arose. And then what would happen to the reputation of Marjorie's Lingerie, that I have spent thirty-two years building up? We would become known as the lingerie store that does not plan, the lingerie store that does not deliver on its promises. Not only that, but what if someone else designed a bra mask of their own to rival the original inventors? Of course that would happen. But would the competition among manufacturers become vicious? Oh I am in a fever of worry now, in which I start muddling up the things that need worrying about. It's not the bra mask I should be devoting my worry too now; it's the flu shots. Because back when I was a kid, Dr. Sabin came out with another polio vaccine, a live virus one, and that was distributed a few years after Dr. Salk's went into circulation, and although Salk was okay with Sabin, Sabin hated Salk. Wouldn't it be awful if that happened with swine flu, if two different kinds of vaccine came out and the inventors came into conflict with each other, even though ultimately everyone wanted the same thing—to make sure people don't get sick? By now I am so worked up I am in my middle-of-the-night cycle of drinking chamomile tea, almost falling asleep, discovering a new angle and fixating, almost falling asleep again, needing a bathroom break, having more tea et cetera.

When I get to Marjorie's Lingerie the next morning, though, I have strangely high energy and optimism, when you consider that I had hardly slept or had a peaceful moment all night long. And before we have been open even half an hour, Barbara Sawchuk comes in, to let me know that Tracey is out of danger; she beat that flu, and she and the baby will leave hospital tomorrow.

"I prayed to Saint Martin and in his compassion, he came through for me," she says.

"Thank God," I say. "But why Saint Martin in particular?"

"Oh well, he's big in France and I'm French on my mother's side, so I grew up admiring him and as a kid I couldn't hear that cloak story enough times."

"How does it go?"

"Well, Martin is travelling on horseback when he comes across a naked pauper who is freezing. He dismounts, cuts his cozy cloak down the centre, and throws half of it over the poor man's shoulders. Then he rides off wearing the other half."

"Beautiful," I say. "Same principle as the bra mask."

"What's that?" she asks. But she is too excited to wait for an answer and goes back to talking about her family.

So Barbara believes St. Martin intervened, and the doctors probably think modern medicine made the difference for Tracey, but I know better. I know I worried her well.

Elixir

COOL DOWN. WORK WITH me. Drink, pee, let me dab that head. Forget your problem with shampoo; this is different. A couple of swabs on the noggin with a damp cloth, and that's it. No soapstung eyeballs tonight. No shocking rinses.

Stop, please. Stop stiffening up, arching your back, showing your fists. I am not the enemy.

How about you redirect your grit? If I sink into a stare or start to snore, I want you to swing into action. Switch into emergency mode. Crank up the siren. Shriek me back into this project.

Over thirty hours running on adrenalin, the caregiver's elixir. Plus coffee that's lost its power through heavy consumption. Must find a new stupor-breaking substance.

Coming up to midnight now. Thirty-two hours and seven minutes since the trip to Emergency. Critical to track time precisely. The project demands precision. Keep up the mantra: we've got control. This fever is not in charge.

The doctor at Emergency kept his voice level, like they must have taught him to do, but worried eyes gave him away. A young guy. Likely a resident. Used a revolutionary approach—treated me as an equal. Said he wanted to keep you in hospital, Bellybutton, but he couldn't, for lack of beds. Told me to prepare mentally for a big project. Recited the grocery list for your care: antibiotics, frequent cooling baths, drops for fever reduction, drinks. "Make sure she pees," he said, "and I suggest you keep the room cool."

Okay. Window's open. But how does a person make sure another person pees?

He wrote on the prescription pad, tore off the little paper, handed it to me. No chicken scratch; he had printed. What was wrong with this doctor?

"It'll be tough, but you'll need to keep up the drill until the fever breaks," he said. He spared me the trouble of asking the next question. "Can't say how long it'll take. I'd suggest you and her father take shifts, even bring in a third person to help if you can. This is slogging work."

Your father? The one who departed while you were still a fish swimming around in a water-filled gourd? Not likely we'll be running into him on the caregiving circuit.

No, Bellybutton, it's you and me and that's it; an all-girl duo.

"But it can't be life-threatening." I spoke declaratively, as though stating a fact.

"I'm afraid it is." The well-trained voice stayed strong and even. It's those eyes he's got to work on.

Here, have a swig of juice now. Pretend you're a drink-and-pee doll. Let's check that diaper. Still dry? We can't have that. Do your business. Doctor's orders.

We'll go all night again if we have to, we'll go all day tomorrow, we'll go until we no longer know how long we've been going and time bends into itself and we get lost in the folds.

Stop. We will not do any of that. We will keep counting minutes and hours, keep moving toward the next sunrise.

Asleep again. In this state, you remind me of the coming-out. Remember that party? Big pains; pokey progress; pictures of my insides, both of us refusing to smile. Later, cut, cut, cut; scoop out the round-headed one. A fish no more.

Awake. Check your underarm temperature. Still high. Into my arms now. Let's head for the can, run a cooling bath, bring that mercury down. Let's wipe down that head again. This fever is not in charge.

Oxymoronic

I MIGHT AS WELL be a pure-bred bitch, the way my mother puts me on show when we're out together. "Listen to how Lisa expresses herself, just like an adult. You'd never guess she's seventeen, would you?" And this is what I got last week from my mother's friend Trish: "Oh Lisa, I hear you got another award at school, how lovely, you should be proud, but you could afford to put on a couple of pounds, feed your body as well as your brain, and do you ever get out and have fun? You're such a serious girl."

And you, madam, are a serious idiot. Mumble, run away.

My mother and her inane friends are rarely around me, though, and that's just fine with me. Over the past few years I have gradually discovered that I don't need people. Except, of course, for Cayden, my sanity saver.

On Thursday afternoons Cayden and I cut classes so we can really spend a good block of time together. I should write a book and call it *Thursdays with Cayden*. I could make a killing, get onto Oprah, the whole bit. Usually, since we are both penniless grade twelve students, we go to Eduardo's, this tiny café on Seventeenth

Avenue, an easy walk from school, somewhat west of Fourteenth Street, out of the bustle zone and Red Mile territory. Hardly anyone comes in, and the place is spotless, which is important to both of us. There's original art on the bathroom walls and the staff are accepting. They let us order spearmint tea and nothing else and sit there for hours, and they don't make us feel guilty.

Whatever else we talk about, two topics are bound to come up: books, and whether Cayden should tell his parents.

Along with our school stuff, we've always got the books we are currently reading, or some of them, and our journals. We may stop talking for half an hour or more at any point to read or write. Right now Cayden is working on *The Selfish Gene*, by Richard Dawkins. I'm on my third reading of *Moby Dick*, which has a why-are-we-here quality that keeps calling me back. This time around, I'm skipping the parts on whale biology and blubber processing. Quaint as they are, those chapters won't help me solve my problem. What I need to figure out is why Captain Ahab's own life and his crew's lives are less important to him than offing one stupid white whale. Is that why we exist? To give expression to the power of hate?

After our book chatter, Cayden and I talk again about his agonizing dilemma. At some point he will have to come out to his parents. A day will come when he wants to invite his significant other to the family home for Christmas dinner, and that significant other is male. Then what?

"I should get it over and done with, shouldn't I?" he asks. "I should just tell them, and see what happens."

"My opinion hasn't changed since last Thursday," I say.

"Tell me why again. Why should I tell them?"

"To put an end to the debate inside your head, which is driving you crazy. And to wake them up. Finally they'll have to pay attention. They'll have to acknowledge you exist."

"I'm not sure I want them to wake up, if it's just to hate me. Being gay is not exactly the norm in a conservative Scots-Canadian family."

"You mean, being openly gay. Anyway, if they react badly it'll be because they're conservative. Nothing to do with national origins."

"Whatever. I'm not going to quibble over *why* they'll treat me like shit."

"Point taken. But what if they don't?"

"They will. Anyway, it's all academic unless I find a boyfriend."

"Not unless. Until."

"Oh, Lisa, you're such an optimist." But I'm not. It's simply a fact that Cayden is intelligent, kind, and attractive. What discerning gay male could resist those intense eyes, that impish smile? Yes, he is slightly overweight, but that only adds to his charm, as do his glasses. There's no reason for him to stay single. It may take a while, but once he is on his own, no longer under his parents' roof and thumb, he'll find a suitable guy and they will settle into a happy life together.

That will not be anything like my story. I suspect that I am one of those odd individuals who will never mate, never even date. First of all, I'd be the first to admit that few people my age, or any age, want to have anything to do with me. I'm not sure why; maybe it's my sullenness, my refusal to please. In any case, there is no reason to believe that particular reality will change over time. Secondly, what guy would want to fool around with someone who has an overly sensitive vagina? Yes they are all sensitive, but mine always hurts or tingles or itches. Sometimes I experience a white noise kind of soreness, but other times it's like I've created habitat down there for a colony of killer bees.

How I got this way, I don't know. But surely a man's testosterone-driven urges would push him to find a potential lifemate, or even a temporary bedmate, with no vaginal disorders whatsoever. Of course, I speak of heterosexual males' motives with only a theoretical understanding, but reading a great deal and being a keen observer must count for something.

Then there is the most sensible reason of all for living a life of abstention. The truth is, the thought of having sex frightens me. I see no options but to stay away from it forever or put up with major pain just to make a man happy. Eating onion rings is enough to cause me significant vaginal pain. What will insertion of a large object do, accompanied with friction and thrust? I don't even like to imagine.

Right now, Cayden is all I need in the way of male

company or any company. I don't have to worry that he will ever come after me. He can talk to me about his insecurities and I can feel useful as I give him advice and encouragement. We have a perfect arrangement. Well, maybe not perfect. But good.

"I've got a physics test tomorrow morning," Cayden says. "Better get home to study."

He lives in Bankview and I'm in Mount Royal so we can walk home together part way. When we say goodbye I feel kind of lonely but it I know it will pass. It happens every Thursday.

I'm starved, forgot to eat lunch again today, so when I get back home I go straight for the chicken. I wish my diet were more varied. To keep me alive, my mother relies heavily on pre-cooked barbecued chicken from Safeway and mixed frozen vegetables. She doesn't have time to cook, due to her killer schedule. She is kind of a professional volunteer, oxymoronic as that sounds. Her days and evenings are jam-packed with board retreats, silent auctions, recognition dinners, visioning sessions. She dresses every day as though she were about to attend an audience with the Queen. Accessories are her passion and chunky gold is her aesthetic. She wears rings, bracelets, necklaces big enough to double as construction tools. As she drives from one do-gooder session to another she talks non-stop on her cellphone. What motivates my mother is the prospect of the next event, the next conference or meeting or gala.

My father's death when I was eleven came out of nowhere. He travelled back and forth frequently to Saudi Arabia on business and on one trip his plane crash-landed in water and some passengers, including my father, didn't make it. He had never learned to swim so that didn't help. I'm not saying my mother was unaffected by his death, although they had always spent a lot of time apart, even when he was in town, and when they were together, they tended to alternate between bickering and fighting hard. But she never went through what would normally be called a grieving process. Right after my father's funeral, she got started on her charity kick, and in the six years she has been on her own, she has never stopped zooming around to her dazzling array of activities.

Maybe it would have been better if my father had not insured himself up the yingyang. If my mother had faced the necessity to do paid work, she would have gone back to the same office day after day and eventually her personal issues would have piled up in her psychological inbox and she would have had to deal with them. Now she can bypass all the real stuff by attaching to a different cause every few minutes.

I don't mind being on my own as much as I am. In the evenings there's a lot of time to reflect and read and, of course, to keep up with my schoolwork. Even on the nutrition front, I'm all right. Eating chicken doesn't bring about vaginal irritation, nor do steamed peas and carrots. The average Safeway chicken lasts me three days. In fairness to my mother, she never forgets to bring in a new bird whenever needed. Maybe she thinks of me as another charity.

I shouldn't speak so harshly of her. She knows I cut classes on Thursday afternoons and she knows why and she is good with it, as long as I keep up my grades, which has never been a problem. And oddly enough, she talks to people about me in glowing terms, as though we were close. When she drags me out to the occasional function, I feel like the trophy daughter. In a way it's infuriating but still, I can see that she's proud of me, and that is comforting.

As far as meals go, my mother could, frankly, put in a little more effort. I once made the mistake of mentioning my vaginal sensitivity to her and my theory that certain foods exacerbated the problem. She blew me off, asked me to prove it. *What?* How does an individual prove the experience of sensation? Are terminal cancer patients required to prove pain before the doctor agrees to prescribe morphine?

After I've finished my homework and am heading off to bed, Cayden calls. He's having a panic attack about his physics test tomorrow. I talk him down, but once I get off the phone, I am too wired to sleep. I'm not in the mood for Captain Ahab's insanity at the moment so I pick up my latest public library acquisition, *Our Knowledge of the External World*, by Bertrand Russell. Logical atomism, sense-data, particles…I don't really get it, but if I read enough of this kind of material, I hope to catch on to its meaning. My goal is nothing less than to work out the riddle of existence.

* * *

Thursday afternoon, and Cayden is pining.

"It's pointless," he says. "Max Lemco is straight."

"How do you know?"

"Well, he's got a girlfriend, for starters."

Poor Cayden. This is not the first time he's fallen for a straight guy.

"Find out about Max's faults. Break the bubble," I say.

"Is that what you do?"

"Well, I'm no expert in such matters...but yes. Yes it is."

"Who are you talking about exactly?" Cayden asks. He's smiling mischievously and that makes me uncomfortable. I don't mind talking to him about his insecurities but am not much inclined to discuss mine. I say nothing for a good five seconds. But in the end, I trust him. "Paul Mercer."

"Him?" Cayden asks, a little more incredulously than I like. "Paul Mercer the redhead genius jock? I didn't know you had a thing for him."

"It's irrelevant. It was two years ago, it's history."

"So...what cured you?"

"Well, you'll recall that he won the grade ten public speaking award for his speech on integrity."

"Yeah, and they took the prize away from him for plagiarism."

"Right. Zachary Plotnick happened to read the article that Paul had lifted that speech from, pretty much word for word. Zach told the principal, and down fell Paul Mercer."

"So...what are you telling me?"

"Cayden, please. You have a great mind. Use it. How can a person love a plagiarist? It was game over for the redhead genius jock and me as soon as the truth came out."

"Game over? But you had never dated him."

"Don't get bogged down in details. I'm giving you a lesson here. A lesson about breaking the bubble. A lesson about liberation. Find out about some reprehensible thing Max Lemco has done and poof, the spell will be broken."

"Okay, I'll give it some thought, although I can't imagine him doing anything reprehensible. Say, do you think I should come out to my parents?"

"My opinion has not changed since last week."

His parents are so far out of touch with who he is, and I'm not just talking about his gayness. His father is a businessman who travels all over the world; in fact, he and my dad knew each other. His mother seems to have an unnatural aversion to her own son. She stays away from home a lot, like my mother does, but at least my mother says nice things about me. As far as his parents are concerned, he might as well not exist.

Like me, Cayden is completely ignorant of the mysteries of cooking. His parents are odd that way. They had ample opportunity to teach him. His father was a cordon bleu chef before he entered the world of high finance, and his mother used to be a recipe tester for the Blue Flame Kitchen. Between the two of them, you'd think they could come up with something more exciting than frozen burritos and reduced fat sour cream for their beloved son's dinners.

Cayden's mother stays away from him with much feebler excuses than my mother's. His mother is a shopper. She takes in every sale, every so-called limited time offer. In the evenings she attends exclusive preferred-shoppers wine and cheese parties at pretentious clothing boutiques, where she can buy the necessities of life such as designer driving gloves. Meanwhile, at the other end of town, Cayden is performing in a classical guitar recital, with no parents present to cheer him on. Only me. Cayden gets panic attacks when stressful situations are coming up, especially exams and concerts. Fear grips him like a vise. His chest tightens, his palms sweat, he gets dizzy, he feels that unknown sinister forces are after him and in a second he will die. He needs reassurance and calming to get back his equilibrium and the only one he gets help from is me. His parents know he suffers and they do nothing. He writes poetry full of big questions and powerful observations. He is the most loyal friend a person could hope for. But none of his qualities or problems even register with his dopey parents.

If I am ever lucky enough to be a mother, you will find me in the audience at every school concert, and by my kid's bedside when he is sick. You won't catch me at the sale of the season or the fundraiser of the decade, not when my kid needs me. As far as I'm concerned, the stores can go out of business and the charities can fold. I will be there for that kid, period. And meals—oh the variety he will enjoy. Nothing frozen, ever. I am going to treat him just the way Cayden and I treat each other. In a way we are each other's parents.

"Why do you worry so much about their reaction," I say. "I mean, your parents already neglect you. Do you think they would even care that you are gay?"

"You can count on it," Cayden says, and I know he's right.

* * *

Today, as soon as we've settled in with our tea, Cayden says, "I met someone."

"Really? That's great, I guess. Is he gay?"

"I think so. I hope so."

"Who is he? Why didn't you tell me about this earlier?"

"Well, why didn't you tell me about Paul Mercer until two years after the fact?"

He's got a point. I don't talk to him about certain things, such as my crushes and my chronic vaginal distress.

It turns out that Jeff, the guy in question, is in second year university, majoring in Political Science. Cayden met him three weeks ago at a public symposium he attended on the politics of the Middle East. He and Jeff happened to be seated next to each other at one of the sessions and got to talking. Since then they have met for coffee a couple of times.

"But come on, how can you tell he's gay?" I ask. I'm persistent when I want to know something. "Did he say so?"

"No."

"Then how do you know?"

"I just do."

"That's not very rational. Anyway, make sure you don't get hurt."

"How am I supposed to do that?" Cayden asks.

* * *

Eduardo's is fuller than usual today. There must be a dozen people in here.

Cayden says that he and Jeff haven't done anything yet. But that's because he's not ready and Jeff is giving him as much time and space as he needs.

"Maybe he's stringing you along," I say.

"Please, Lisa," he says.

He's right. It's just proving to be a little more difficult than I had anticipated to deal with this changing scenario. What's the rush? Can't he continue to live in the world of theoretical gayness for just a year or two longer? Then we can reassess. It's not that I am attracted to Cayden; I'm not. Cayden is my companion, my comrade. And here he is, getting ready to abandon me in favour of romantic love.

"I'm not giving you up," he says, apparently reading my mind. "If this works out, it will be an addition to my life. No way you're getting pushed out by some guy."

He keeps reassuring me, rubs my back. Then he goes

to the counter and gets hot water refills for our tea. I settle down a little and our conversation turns to our latest reading choices, *The Mill on the Floss* for me and *Flatland* for Cayden. Then we come back to the inevitable.

"So I guess it's time I told my parents, eh?"

"Well," I say, "you have new circumstances now."

"So what are you saying? That I should or shouldn't?"

"What do you think?"

* * *

I've been reading a bit on the Internet about straight girls who hang out with gay guys. At one time the term of choice was "fag hag," but then it was felt that the word "fag" could never be anything but offensive. So today, in hip parlance, I would be referred to as a "fruit fly."

These descriptions turn my stomach. What purpose does it serve to create such categories? To make the world seem tidy and comprehensible, when really it is unfathomable? Do we exist in order to classify one another?

* * *

Miraculously, my mother is home on this Wednesday night and she cooks for me. Dinner is a beef stir fry, followed by chocolate mousse topped with whipped cream. I have to admit, it's a tasty change. When the phone rings, I run to get it. It's Cayden.

"Hang on a sec," I say.

I run upstairs with the phone, retreat into my room. I plop onto the bed and sit on it with my knees up.

"I'm back," I say.

"Guess what?"

"Speak."

"I did it," he says.

"What? Does this involve your mother and father or your new boyfriend?"

"Parents." he says. "I told them. Just about me, not about Jeff. That'll come later."

"Wow, that's great Cayden. How'd they take it?"

"They just sat there. My father stared into space. My mother looked at her hands."

"Didn't they say anything?"

"Not really. I guess they're in shock or something. The tension was pretty bad."

"So how do you feel?" I asked.

"Kind of hurt, but no panic attack. I'd rehearsed the scene thousands of times in my head and that's how it went."

"Pretty shabby. Their behaviour, I mean."

"Whatever. It's done now. No more debating."

* * *

Today is not exactly a typical Thursday. Cayden has a dental appointment at noon, so we won't be able to walk to Eduardo's together but he'll catch up with me there later, probably at about two o'clock. That's fine, because I've got a plan that will take a little time to carry out. In my jeans pocket, I've got the cash my mother gave me for my birthday last week. I'm going to head over to my favourite indie bookstore, pick out some new releases for us. Cayden deserves a reward for coming out to his parents. And for carrying out his promise not to abandon me, even though he and Jeff are officially an item now.

Maybe I have earned a reward too, who knows what for. I'll figure that out another time.

Lumps

WHEN I FOUND THE lump, my mother and I were sitting at the kitchen table. She was solving the Monday crossword puzzle in the Montreal Star while I flipped through a library book, trying to figure out how to end my ban-the-bomb speech. I turned the pages with my right hand while rubbing the back of my neck absent-mindedly with my left.

"A lump," I said. "Can you check?"

My mother got up, walked to my side of the table and stood beside me. I guided her hand to the lump. Then she poked around and found another one behind my left ear.

"Do those babies hurt?" she asked.

"Not much. But still."

"Let's go over the facts again," she said. How many times had she used those words in the past five years? And always with patience. I didn't realize at the time what she was giving me. "Your father died of a fast-moving leukemia. It's not contagious. You're a healthy girl. You don't have any kind of cancer."

"But they're lumps," I said.

On TV they had ads showing the five signs of cancer. The number one sign was *a lump or thickening in the breast or elsewhere.* I kept finding lumps and sometimes thickenings. Once I had shown my mother a thickening on the sole of my foot. She explained that it was a callus. I was mad at the people who wrote down those signs of cancer for the ads. They should have told me exactly what they meant by *thickening*.

"Do you feel okay except for the lumps on your head?"

"My throat hurts."

My mother left the room and came back with her medical bible, *Baby and Child Care*, by Dr. Spock.

"What are you doing checking that book? I'm not a two year old."

"Dr. Spock doesn't just give advice about infants and toddlers. I'm sure I can find things in here about thirteen-year-olds too."

"But it's 1961. It's not like, 1948 or whenever the book came out. It's gotta be out of date."

"No, he puts out a new edition every few years and I keep up. Lots of parents do."

She spends a couple of minutes reading. Then she looks up from the book.

"Okay, I have a hunch about what you've got," she says.

"Cancer, right?"

"Not even close."

"So what is it?"

"Look, let's give Dr. Shatsky a shout. He's the expert."

She called Dr. Shatsky's after-hours answering service. Not long after, the doctor phoned her back and she told him my symptoms. She was precise. I think in her heart she would have liked to be a doctor.

"He'll come by later," she said when she got off the phone. "Are we ever lucky he'll make a house call at this hour. I'm sure he'd prefer to relax."

"Oh man, I must be really sick," I said.

"Irene. Look at me. You don't have cancer."

"I thought you said you're not an expert."

"I did too. There's no flies on you, kid," she said, and we both laughed, only she laughed a lot harder than I did.

On the medical side, there was nothing to do but wait, so we went back to our routine. I liked spending time with my mother after supper and cleanup. Usually it was like this, with her reading the paper or solving the crossword puzzle and me doing homework. Brenda Faigelman had called her mother a bitch and moved in with her aunt for three days. With Paula Boland it was worse. She and her mother had gotten into fisticuffs over her curfew and one time Paula wound up needing eleven stitches under her eye. After that she left Montreal and went to live with her grandparents in Buffalo, New York. So many girls I knew were in conflict with their mothers. My mother and I weren't going through any of that. Maybe if my father hadn't died it would have worked out differently; I had been a daddy's girl. But once he was gone, my mother and I gradually grew much closer. She said her mission was to help me grow up strong.

After my father's death, she switched from part-time to full-time at Cuttler Webb, the furniture store where she worked as a bookkeeper. We needed the money and she let me know it, even though I was only eight at the time. I felt grown up knowing about that. Now she spent some of her work hours on the sales floor too. She said that sales was not her first choice but at Cuttler Webb, they treated her like family and it was less complicated for her to just do work for them over and above the bookkeeping, rather than going out to get a second part-time job. Sometimes I think her stories about the furniture store helped me to prepare my mind for my own job so many years later at Marjorie's Lingerie.

My mother had won our first TV set in 1958 when she got the jackpot call on the radio show *A & P Calling*. You mailed your A & P Supermarket receipts in to the show and if they picked your name, they'd call you. Every day there were three chit-chat calls and one jackpot call. You had to answer four questions correctly to win. They happened to call my mother on her day off and I was home from school with a sinus infection. How lucky was that? She sailed through the first three questions. Then they asked her to name the capital of Alaska and she motioned to me to look it up, because nobody told her not to. I ran to our *Webster's Encyclopaedic Dictionary*, did what needed doing, and handed her a one-word note. When our TV arrived, my mother nicknamed it Juneau.

The one show I never missed was *Ben Casey*, which was on at eight o'clock every Thursday night. Having *Ben Casey* to look forward to helped me live through my wretched Thursday afternoon sewing classes. The show began with the words Man, Woman, Birth, Death, Infinity, spoken by old Dr. Zorba, who was wise and had Albert-Einstein hair. In real life Dr. Zorba was married to the glamour puss Bettye Ackerman—Dr. Maggie Graham on the show. But Dr. Casey was the one who razzed my berries. He was a brain surgeon. What looks. What a mind. I couldn't decide whether I wanted him for a replacement father or a boyfriend. I understood him like no other woman could. Even though he had so much going for him, I could tell he was hurting. In one episode Joan Hackett played his patient and they fell for each other, which I thought was wrong and a cheap thing to do. It wasn't Dr. Casey's fault though. She went after him from her hospital bed. Sick as she was, she still had the energy to flirt with her brain surgeon. In the last moments of the show she asked him, "Do…all your patients fall in love with you?" Then she died.

But this was Monday, not a great TV night, and Dr. Shatsky would be arriving soon. Anyway, I had to get back to work. I wanted to find a great quote to end my speech. The debate was coming up on Thursday.

I decided to talk to my mother about it. She hadn't finished high school but that was only because when she was fifteen she had to go to work in a button factory to help support her family. Later on she went to business college, which was where she had learned bookkeeping. She read all the time, especially life stories. Sometimes on her day off she would meet me after school and we would take three buses to the Fraser-Hickson Library so she could borrow more biographies. I was more of a magazine reader, even then. While my mother got the straight dope on Madam Curie and Galileo, I was content to read about Natalie Wood and her kid sister Lana in *Calling All Girls.* Doing research about nuclear disarmament was a stretch for me.

"I'm asking for the United States and England to stop making and testing nuclear weapons right now, to set a good example for Russia," I said. "I want to finish the speech with the words of a famous ban-the-bomb person. Maybe Bertrand Russell."

"Why him?" my mother asked.

"Because I've been reading about him and he used to be the president of the CND."

"The what?"

"The Campaign for Nuclear Disarmament."

"Oh."

"And now he heads up the Committee of One Hundred."

"So who are the other ninety-nine?"

"They're like—they think the CND are slowpokes."

"I see. All right. So you want to quote Bertrand Russell, the philosopher?"

"Yeah, Mommy. That's the guy. What's wrong?"

"I read something about him too," my mother said. "It seems that years ago, he told his wife he was heading out on a bike ride. It turned out to be a long trip, with lots of stops to do whatever philosophers do. He never returned home."

"So what? He still wants world peace."

"But what if that personal story is true?" my mother said. "At least he could have talked to her first instead of just riding off like that. He could have said, 'So long, keep well, I won't be back.' Can't you quote some other famous person?"

"Maybe Linus Pauling. Above-ground nuclear testing drives him nuts. Or I could take something from Albert Schweitzer. His speech, 'The Problem of Peace' is in my library book. The whole thing."

"Schweitzer—now there's a gentle person. You know what I heard about him? He's left-handed, but if a cat is resting against his left arm and he has to write something, he'll do the writing with his right hand, just so as not to disturb the cat."

"Okay, Schweitzer is the one."

"Wait. I've got an even better idea. Go for the best—Benjamin Spock. He's in the peace movement."

Her and her Dr. Spock.

* * *

It took Dr. Shatsky one minute to make his diagnosis: German measles.

"I knew it," my mother said.

The lumps were swollen lymph glands, he said. I should expect a rash, which would disappear in a few days. I might also develop cold symptoms to go with my sore throat.

"For now, you can watch Howdy Doody and Mighty Mouse on television. No school for seven days," he said.

"But I have to give a speech on Thursday," I said.

"Childhood diseases show up at inconvenient times. I've noticed that," he said.

After Dr. Shatsky left I cried. Then I stomped through the kitchen, across the long hall to the living room and back. After doing the circuit a couple a few times, I could hear Madame Lemieux downstairs rapping on her ceiling with her broomstick. I'd heard that sound often enough before. My mother phoned her and said, "Cecile, I'm sorry. Irene's been kicking a disappointment out of her system. It'll stop now."

I told my mother I would not let the debate go ahead without me. I'd ask Dr. Foster to move the date.

"Well, what's the harm in asking?" my mother said.

* * *

On Tuesday morning the rash surfaced, starting on my face and working its way down to my neck. By the time I got up the nerve to phone the school it had reached my chest. Miss Johanssen, the school secretary, said that Dr. Foster was teaching, but she'd have him call me back at recess. She said she was sorry I wasn't feeling well. Miss Johanssen was kind to everyone. Just before Paula Boland left for Buffalo, Miss Johanssen gave her a matching birthstone necklace and ring set. Miss Johanssen had redeemed all her Pinky stamps at Steinberg's Supermarket to get the set; that's how much she cared about Paula.

Dr. Foster was the teacher in charge of the debating club, so I figured he had to be the one with the power to change the date of the big debate. Our whole season had built up to the final debate that was coming up on Thursday. After four elimination rounds, this is what it shook down to: Joline Proulx and me against Morris Kochinski and Linda Freedman in a showdown on nuclear disarmament, with the whole school looking on. Morris and Linda were going to argue that the Russians would blow us all up if the United States and Britain listened to Joline and me.

I told Dr. Foster why we needed to change the date. He said no; he had to respect Mr. Durocher's schedule. (Durocher was the big shot downtown lawyer who was coming to the school to judge the debate.) Also, everyone was expecting that the debate would go ahead on Thursday, Dr. Foster said. It was not for him to disrupt plans that had been finalized. He'd ask Myra Gottlieb to take my place. There was no time for her to write a new speech, so he'd drive over to my home during lunch hour today to pick up my speech. Myra would deliver the speech but I would be given credit for writing it.

Dr. Foster sounded sure of himself, like a master commanding his dog to roll over.

"No," I said.

"Be reasonable, Irene," he said.

"Then you be fair," I said.

"This is a fair solution. Think about it. And I'll be over at twelve-ten."

"I won't tell you my address."

"That's quite all right. The school keeps records."

* * *

At one o'clock I heard from my mother.

"Mr. Foster called me here at work," she said.

"It's Doctor."

"Pardon?"

"Doctor Foster, not Mister. He's got a doctor of philosophy degree in history, he could have a university post, and yet he chose to teach children just entering adolescence. That's his speech when he's fed up with us."

"Doctor. Fine. He just called himself Jeremy Foster. How could I be expected to figure out his whole life with no clues? Anyway, he's coming back to the house after I get home. No more Bette Davis performances, please. This time, hand over the speech, okay?"

"Mommy, he's a creep."

"Then you should feel sorry for him, because he probably hasn't got any friends. That's not the point."

"But the speech is mine. I don't even want Winston Churchill to deliver it."

"Churchill can live with the disappointment," my mother said. "Foster won't let up until he gets what he wants."

She promised she would try to come home earlier than usual so that we could talk.

* * *

By the time she got back, at about half past four, the rash had spread down to my abdomen and was itchy. I was exhausted, my head ached, my throat was so raw I had trouble swallowing. I was also dejected, because I realized by now that I really would have to say goodbye to my dream of delivering my own speech.

My mother called the school, asked for Dr. Foster. She told him we'd need a little more time. Could he come over at about six o'clock? He agreed to that. People didn't usually say no to my mother. They responded to her honesty.

"First of all, let's take care of what ails you," she said. She boiled up a bit of oatmeal, ladled it into a clean dishtowel, and tied the towel up into something that looked like Charlie Chaplin's hobo pack. Then she ran me a bath and rubbed the porridge pack gently over my skin to ease the itching. Once I was out of the tub, she heated up a pot of Campbell's vegetarian vegetable soup and served me a bowl of it, along with a weak cup of Red Rose tea.

I started to feel better.

Then, my mother sat down at the kitchen table and faced me.

"All right, go to town," she said.

"What do you mean? I'm not allowed out."

"Tell me why justice is not being done—why you feel it's wrong that Myra Gottlieb will give your speech."

I told her that Myra Gottlieb might pick up German measles bugs from the sheets of foolscap I had written the speech on. Then she would transmit the disease to Joline and soon it would spread through the school like wildfire.

My mother said she was proud of me for being so civic minded, but she didn't think the bugs could live on paper, or at least not long enough to infect Myra. Anyway, if Myra did, through some miracle, get infected, and pass the disease on to other girls, they would be spared from getting it years later in pregnancy. German measles could be bad news for a baby in the womb. So by hand-ing over infected papers, I could help every other girl in the school.

"Nobody should be allowed to deliver another person's speech. It's stealing."

"But wouldn't it different if you were given credit for it?" my mother asked. "I mean, when Myra gets up to give the speech, she'll explain that you wrote the words. As long as she does that, how is it wrong?"

"I worked so hard. I don't want to miss out."

"Okay, name a disease that needs a cure."

"Cancer."

"So let's say you're a research scientist and you discover a cure for cancer, but then you find out that you're dying of something else and have two days to live. Will you hide your cancer cure from the world because you'll miss out on the glory?"

"But I'm crazy about my speech."

"That's a mother's love. It's not healthy to be together all the time. Let your baby go for an outing with Auntie Myra."

"Mommy," I said, "you should be in the debating club."

It was ten to six. I went to my bedroom, got the speech from under my pillow, brought it to the kitchen, and set it down on the table. I decided I would let myself have one last read-through before the handover.

When Dr. Foster arrived, my mother poured him a cup of coffee and I behaved like a human being. No more drama.

"Read my ending," I said to him. "Read it out loud.

Please. I really like my ending."

He reached into the breast pocket of his jacket and got out his glasses. Then he flipped to the last page and read, but not out loud.

"Schweitzer," he said. "Interesting choice. Personally, I might have been inclined to go with Russell."

Renovations

I'VE BEEN BUILDING UP to this moment since I was ten. That's when I started developing, right side only. The breast grew quickly and created serious problems for me. People had been taking shots at me at school for being short and thin. Now the comments were even more piercing. Football jokes. Watermelon cracks. I'd run home from school crying, escape into my room.

My mother took me to the doctor to make sure nothing was wrong. He told us that in some girls, the breasts mature one at a time. I tried to tell the kids at school I was normal, but they weren't in a listening mood.

Eventually the left side caught up. But because of my small frame, the breasts looked enormous. Right through junior high and high school, the comments continued; they just took a different form. Samantha Dickson dubbed me Miss Ten Minutes. The idea was that if I was approaching you, you'd see my breasts first and the rest of me would follow ten minutes later. The name stuck.

At sixteen I read about breast reduction surgery and told my mother about it. She wouldn't let me get it done; she worried about regrets later on.

When I was at university, I met a medical student, Zack. He invited me out for afternoon coffee—a safe first date—or so I thought. As soon as we sat down, he said, "Alyssa, do you realize your right breast is slightly bigger than your left? Doesn't that bother you?" I walked out of the café stifling sobs, spent the next two days in my room.

After graduation, I started up an accounting practice. My time and energy went into the work. By the time I reached my mid-twenties, business was booming. Then, at a mutual funds conference, I met Jeff, an actuary. I was sick of guys who spent entire evenings staring at my breasts and entire nights manhandling them. It wasn't like that with Jeff. We took long walks, haunted bookstores, talked about art, politics, everything. In bed he was gentle, not fixated like the others. I actually stopped worrying about the breast thing.

Until we finally got married.

Jeff underwent a transformation, like some sort of perverse magic was at work. He zoomed in on the breasts and that's where he stayed. The rest of myself, even my body, didn't exist for him.

For a year I stuck it out, every night reliving the date with Zack, flashing back to fifty other dates with breast-obsessed guys. I tried to talk to Jeff about it, but he was no longer interested in talking to me. Why talk when you can bite and squeeze and suck until a person's nipples hurt?

When I finally got up the nerve to leave the marriage,

I chose abstinence. For the past ten years, I've stayed away from men. Often I get lonely, but the relative peace is worth it.

The doctor is here now. Doctor Althauser. Big-boned but small-breasted. I wonder if she's had the operation. After a few minutes of small talk she says, "I need to do some measuring and marking, if I may."

She works a narrow tape measure over the breasts. Then she draws lines on them with a thick black pen. At the midpoint in the cleavage she makes a tiny x.

"I do the before and after circles now," she says. "The befores surround the nipples in their present position. The afters mark the spots where we'll be reinserting the nipples."

There are vast distances between the befores and afters. I feel oddly detached from my body, as though I'm watching a house getting prepped for renovations.

Soon after Dr. Althauser leaves, a young technician comes in. She tries to get an intravenous needle into my arm but she can't find the vein. "You have rolling veins," she says, and tries again. The third attempt works.

Every ten minutes or so I have to pee. This is just how I used to get before exams at school. It's quite a production, wheeling the IV pole down to the other end of my room and into the bathroom. I fall back on my usual strategy for getting through a bad moment—lining up all my reasons for being where I am. It's not just the problems with men. It's the back pain. It's the difficulty in finding clothes that fit. It's the endless, fruitless search for a bra that does the job without leaving angry red marks on my shoulders and a rash on my chest from underwire irritation.

Shopping trip. In a clothing store, I overhear a conversation between a salesclerk and a customer. The customer is in front of the mirror, sporting a bright red turtleneck and black leggings, price tags sticking out of the backs of the garments.

"This is great," the customer says. "Since my breast reduction, I'm the same size top and bottom."

"How did you decide to go through with it?" the clerk asks. The clerk is large-breasted.

"I had a baby and couldn't nurse him for lack of milk," the customer says. "That's what convinced me to get the surgery done. Knowing that my huge, heaving tits weren't doing anyone any good—couldn't even bring in a food supply for my kid."

"I hear the operation makes you lose sensation in the nipples," the clerk says.

"Not for me," the customer says. "I had feeling back right away."

This is the crystallizing moment for me. I know now that I will go ahead.

My surgery isn't scheduled until noon. I've never been a big eater but I'm having trouble with the pre-op fast. I see myself eating an enormous Greek salad, sucking the juice out of every black olive. Then a souvlaki, dripping with lamb juice, and dipped in a smooth plain yogurt. I don't care about the surgery any more. I need to eat.

A nurse comes in to give me a shot. "To relax you," she says. Usually I ask about medication, but not this time. I don't want to know what's in the syringe.

Time to go. An orderly has arrived with a wheeled cot. Not like in my fantasies of the moment, where there's a stretcher with an attendant at each end. Guess I've seen too many old war flicks.

The orderly babbles to me about hockey scores. I don't know what he's talking about.

Down the elevator, into the operating room. Five or six masked people in jade green scrubs. Running around. What are they so busy with? Lights everywhere, blaring, screaming. From one green creature, "Hi, I'm the anaesthetist." What does he want? It has to do with signing a paper, doesn't it? I signed a paper before. Wait…I have questions…a taste, a weird taste…chemical…powdered cleanser…I taste…I…

"When is the surgery?" I say. The taste is gone, the taste of an instant before.

"You're in the recovery room."

Now I become aware of searing pain. Stab wounds.

In retrospect, I realize I shouldn't have pushed myself so hard so soon after the operation. Back to the office in three days, took up my volunteer charity work a couple of evenings after that. I tried to make like nothing had happened, but when you can't lift your arms over your head and you're covered chest to back in bandages, well, let's face it, something has happened. I wound up with an infected incision, a morning in hospital, antibiotics. Thank God, the pain has gone now. Pretty good for only two weeks after surgery.

I awake on a Saturday morning after a fitful night. I'm sweating, agitated. I don't like the sounds coming through the window, invading my narrow space. A magpie cackles in the poplar. A truck screeches around the corner.

I get up, rush into the bathroom, take deep breaths in the tub, like I learned years ago in a yoga class. It's no use. Incisions all show. The nipples are shaped wrong. They're supposed to be round, subtle. These ones come to ridiculous points, like dog noses.

Breathe in calm, breathe out nerves, breathe in calm, feel the calm…Wait a minute, I still don't have proper sensation, and it's been three months. Paralyzed snouts.

I dress, put on my relaxation CD, Pachelbel's Canon in D with ocean sounds in the background. Lie down and listen. Quieter now. Listen to the waves lapping on the beach. Breasts up, sentinels at attention guarding the beachfront. Against what?

Closing bash for this year's leprosy relief campaign. In all my years of canvassing for charities, it's the first time I've gone to a volunteer recognition event. I figured, it's time.

I bought myself a new dress for this night, form-fitting, navy velvet. I'm a little looser than usual; I've had a couple of glasses of red wine. They push back the tables after the meal and the DJ sets up. People get up to dance.

I stand up, walk onto the floor, start moving to the music, making my own dance, and after three, four songs, I realize, hey, I'm dancing braless.

Granny Greens

MABEL HAD A MASSIVE heart attack and died while transferring the contents of her brown purse into her black one. Since then, I only carry one, a navy one.

I get a half-full can of cat food out of the fridge and bend over slowly to fill Mehitabel's bowl. She's getting all matted again. Never should have let Mabel talk me into a longhair.

Mabel's son-in-law came around with his brother this morning. A little round guy about fifty, and a tall skinny one, same age. Mutt and Jeff. They started working me over again about Mabel's will. She had a thing about debt—couldn't stand even the idea of it. She paid bills as soon as they arrived. Even a two-day delay would drive her crazy. So she didn't leave any debts. Eighty percent of her dough she left to the SPCA, and the rest to me. Well, it's no grand fortune but her daughters are furious. They were counting on big bags of cash from the old lady. Both of them have kids in university and live way beyond their means to impress God only knows who. The round little husband is a waste, and the other girl is divorced, and neither one of those daughters ever lifted a finger for

Mabel. Mutt and Jeff asked me to give up my share of the will or things could get ugly, they said. Meanwhile, they're sitting at *my* table drinking tea out of *my* Royal Doulton cups. No dice, I told them, see you in court if it has to be that way. And I asked them to leave. Mehitabel hissed at the tall one. Bless her—what a lovely touch. She got a cat treat for that.

* * *

Funny how two stubborn old crones can hit it off. We were so tight, Mabel and me, that people always assumed we'd known each other for a lifetime. But we only met five years ago, at the library. We were both biography buffs and oddly enough, we were both looking for Irving Stone's book on Lincoln's wife. Well, we got to talking in the stacks and there were two copies of the book. We exchanged phone numbers and arranged to chat when we finished the book. That was how it started and within two months she'd moved out of her depressing little basement apartment and into my house. We talked about everything. Sometimes we bickered over trivia like whose turn it was to cook, but our quarrels never lasted long. It was like a marriage really, and a damn sight more satisfying than the one I had with Jack.

A couple of years ago, we were out for tea and got to talking about how we'd gotten through the change of life. With me, headaches were the main thing, plus night sweats at times. Mabel told me she'd had heavy depression, and her husband was clueless. Mine too. In our day, the men we lived with weren't tuned in. You put up with your symptoms and shut up. So Mabel muddled through, not wanting to live from one day to the next but never letting on. Holiday time was the worst. She'd paste on her hostess smile, bake those Santa cookies, prepare elaborate dinners for twelve, chase after kids on peppermint-cane induced highs, all the time thinking of ways to do herself in.

* * *

I'm in the kitchen fixing my bedtime hot milk when Mabel walks in and sits down in her usual place facing the window.

"Can I have one too?" she asks casually.

"Of course." I reach over for the milk carton and start pouring more into the pot. Then my gut tightens. I look at her. She looks fine.

"Mabel?"

"Yes?" Her tone is matter-of-fact.

"Why are you here?"

"I live here."

"But you died a while ago."

"Nonsense. How's the milk coming?" She leers at me this time, gets up and starts walking toward me. I scream.

How many times will this dream get me in its many forms? For the past week it's been every night. Dead-alive Mabel brushing her hair in her bedroom, doing her lipstick in the bathroom, reading *Love is Eternal* in the living room, using the computer at the library, drinking tea at the supermarket cafeteria. She gets around, this creepy dream-Mabel.

* * *

Tonight I'm going to return to our book club for the first time since Mabel passed. She always had mixed feelings about that group. She loved reading the books and getting her comments ready, but she sometimes found the meetings tedious. She liked to shake it up a bit. One time, she turns to Alex, who's the biggest prude in creation, and she says, "So how did you like the way the author handled that cunnilingus scene? Turn you on?" Alex lost the power of speech and, when we left, Mabel declared the meeting a success.

So many times I've needed to talk to her in the three months she's been gone. I've taken to consulting her inside my head. She hasn't given me a choice really. Tonight, the Mabel inside my head is in no mood for that book club. She wants action.

* * *

Now, here's a change from your run-of-the-mill church. The minister supposedly can read your mind and contact whoever you want to talk to in the great beyond. Plus, she can see into the future. Wow. A young man sits behind a desk in the foyer and hands me a piece of notepaper. I'm to write three questions inside for the minister to answer, then fold the paper and put my initials on the outside. This is stupid, I know it's stupid, but I go ahead with it. I write "1. How is Mabel? 2. What does she need? 3. What will I do?" The Mabel inside my head is laughing out loud. I fold the paper and print my initials on it, then drop it in the box where the young man is collecting the papers.

The meeting hall is just a bare room, with maybe sixty people sitting in rows in grey folding chairs. Facing them, two women and a man sit on a stage unadorned except for a white wooden cross, about three feet tall, bordered all around by pink peonies. The scene is like a nightmare version of an elementary school Remembrance Day assembly. I don't know anyone.

They start with hymns: "Nearer My God to Thee" and "Rock of Ages." Pretty well everybody sings. Then the blonde fiftyish woman on the platform takes in a deep breath, and starts to speak reproachfully in a strange, tinny voice. She does look like she's in a trance, staring straight ahead. She makes a few references to "my vessel" and I figure out she's acting as the vessel for a spirit—the one she sucked in with that deep breath. This spirit is mighty ticked at all of us for being too self-centred and materialistic. The tirade goes on for about ten minutes. Then the woman purses her lips and exhales and the spirit whooshes out. The woman slumps in her chair, exhausted. The man next to her puts his arm around her shoulders gently for a moment. She nods and smiles at him.

Then he begins to talk. This medium is different. He doesn't seem to go into a trance, yet he is supposedly in touch with people on the other side or in transition, which is your trip from the physical to the spirit world. Mabel and I did some reading on this stuff last year for a hoot, so I can sort of follow now. "There you go," says the Mabel in my head, "research always pays off." The man brings direct messages from loved ones to members of the congregation. "Evan, David remembered your birthday. He sends his love, and suggests you re-evaluate that plan to move to Ottawa…Katrina, your neighbour appreciates the extra kindness you showed her husband and son at the funeral…Isabelle, uncross your arms, please; you're blocking a message your grandmother is trying to send…"

He goes on this way for a while, then invites us all to "send out thoughts" so our people on the other side will know we still care for them. I send out thoughts to Mabel even though the Mabel inside my head is still doubled over laughing. It's confusing. I wait for a sign but spirit-Mabel won't come out of hiding. Am I beginning to buy this banana oil or what?

Now it's the minister's turn. She's a large woman, wide and big-framed, and no spring chicken. The young man who greeted me at the entrance brings her the box of papers and she pulls them out one by one, answering the questions.

"Who's HGC?"

"That's me." I talk a little louder than usual, trying to hide my nerves.

"Are you a professor?"

"No."

"But I see you surrounded by books. Big reader?"

"Yes."

"That's it then. You first wanted to know about your friend, right?"

"Yes."

"I'm not quite getting her name. Myrtle, or…Muriel?"

"Mabel."

"Ah. Well, she wants you to know the transition was smooth and she's feeling fine. She doesn't need a thing."

The Mabel in my head shakes her head back and forth gravely. What am I supposed to do now? Who's the real Mabel?

"Your other question…you'll carry on. She'll help you through."

Cold comfort that, when the Mabel in my head is doing what she used to call her Madonna shtik, making a face as she sticks her thumb into a wide-open mouth.

* * *

What'll I do with those granny greens? I can't bear to wear them.

When Mabel took up aerobics I refused to join. No way other people were going to see big chunks of my body, especially in motion. Even the doctors, I don't like them monkeying around between the shoulders and knees. Not Mabel. The heart doctor said to do more exercise and she chose to do it in style. She went to the sport specialty shop and bought spandex leggings—one purple pair, one pink, and her favourites, the bright lime ones she called granny greens. For the top, she picked up snug sleeveless little jerseys with slogans printed on them, like "Don't get sucked into liposuction."

I didn't go to the gym with Mabel, so I never got to see the clothes on her. After she'd been taking the classes for a few weeks, I asked her to model the granny greens for me. I got the camera out and Mabel struck poses for me in the living room. "Pretty good legs for a geezer, eh?" she said with an exaggerated wink.

The next day I bought myself a pair of granny greens, just for around the house. I wore them a lot. I had them on when she died.

I had a neighbour come and gather Mabel's clothes into bags and leave them by the front door. Then I called the women's shelter and asked them to pick up the bags next day. I couldn't touch the clothes or have them around. The same thing happened when my mother died years ago. My aunt had to deal with the clothing. I tried to pick up Mother's straw hat and wound up throwing up all over it. My aunt donated everything to the Sally Ann, which was what gave me the idea for Mabel's stuff.

It occurred to me to put my own granny greens into one of the bags, but I couldn't do that. For now, they sit in the second drawer of my dresser and bother me.

* * *

I'm having a return to the piercing headaches I got during menopause. The Mabel inside my head pulls her macho routine—how, if I don't think about the pain, it will go away. How living with pain builds character and puts hair on your chest. How old age is not for the faint of heart. I'm trying to figure out if there's a pattern to these headaches. Today, it was Mutt and Jeff who started it. Mehitabel tipped me off. Perched on the window sill, she arched her back and let out a good loud hiss. I looked outside and sure enough it was the two of them. This time I didn't let them in. The chatty round one started the usual gripe from the other side of the door. I heard snippets—enough to shoot my blood pressure up twenty, thirty points. Mehitabel wanted blood. Lucky for them she was on my side of the door.

* * *

One of our favourite pastimes was story time. Mabel named the ritual; she said at our age we had an obligation to prove Shakespeare right and revert to our childhood. Almost every evening, after clearing the dinner dishes, we'd sit in the living room with our tea and read out loud from all kinds of books. We'd do everything—*The Diviners,* Milton Acorn's poems, a study of Sri Lankan culture, Leonard Cohen. We'd take turns. I always looked forward to Mabel's turn, especially with the novels. She was such an actress, putting on different voices and mannerisms for the different characters. Once I'd heard Mabel reading, I'd always hear the characters' voices that way in my head. Of course, we did lots of biographies—Madame Curie, Alphonse Desjardins, John Diefenbaker, Margaret Sangster.

We went through a stage where we decided to find out what was going on in business literature, so we read lessons on total quality management. That was the closest we ever came to boring each other.

"Snap out of it," the Mabel in my head orders. "You sound like a B movie."

* * *

Mabel works the crowd like a veteran politician. She stops and talks for a moment with some; others just get the warm, toothy smile. She gently squeezes outstretched hands. Slowly she makes her way to the front of the ballroom. The ornate chandeliers cast a muted light. I am far away, standing against the back wall, enraged. I feel her wielding complete power over them. She reaches her destination, stands behind a dais, and extends her arms, palms out, like the Pope. The crowd cheers. People weep. "You're a fraud!" I cry out, and wake up.

* * *

Tonight in book club we were talking about a new biography of Henry Miller. Alex said, "Where's Mabel when you need her?" I lost it, started screaming that Mabel was gone and couldn't we just get on with it. We had tea and I shut up.

* * *

Stopped off at the market today. Picked up three nectarines, four apples, a bag of rice, a small generic fibre supplement, and bath oil. It's taken almost half a year, but I'm getting the knack of buying for one person again. Met Alex for coffee this afternoon. He's convinced me to join his social justice club, kind of a grey power group. Agreed to go to the next meeting, just to watch. No promises.

* * *

Mabel sits next to me at the movie theatre. We're sharing

a huge tub of popcorn, joking around as we wait for the show to start. We're licking melted butter off our fingers and smacking our lips loudly like bratty kids. Mabel's T-shirt has a picture of the premier with the caption, "Wind Warning: He's About to Open His Mouth." We've got our legs up on the backs of the empty seats in front of us. We're wearing our granny greens.

Corn

IN THE MIDDLE OF the 9 a.m. newscast I have to leave for work, which is a shame. They've just started a story on a heroic rescue in New York. Something about a subway train.

At a quarter after eleven, Sandra di Angelico walks into the store. Her hands are shaking; her breathing is fast and shallow. Nerves.

"What on earth—let's get you seated, Sandra. Take a load off."

I grab a chair from a fitting room, carry it into our back office and return to the front counter where Sandra stands. We're well staffed this afternoon at Marjorie's Lingerie, so I don't have to worry about coverage on the sales floor. I place my hand lightly on Sandra's shoulder and we walk into the office, where I help her into the spare chair from the fitting room. Then I sit in the desk chair and swivel it over to her so that we sit side by side. I take her hand. Her nails dig into my flesh but that's okay, I don't mind a little discomfort when I am helping a person through something.

Her eyes are open as wide as they will go, they dart around like she's trapped, looking for escape. She is so worked up now I can see she has moved on to a whole new level. She's afraid of her fear, afraid of herself.

When my best friend Doreen got like this, she only had one thought. I learned how to help.

"It's okay, Sandra," I say, "you are not going to die. You're safe."

In a few seconds the breathing changes. She inhales deeply, coughs, coughs again. She sucks in so hard it startles her and then she starts making choking sounds. I can see in her face that the fear is rising again.

"You'll be fine. Don't worry. You'll get your breath back," I say.

Asthma, allergies, lung diseases—all kinds of medical conditions can make a person's breathing go haywire. But I saw Doreen through many panic attacks years ago and I can see the signs now in Sandra. I'm unafraid of her crazy breathing. My job is to help her be unafraid too.

Once the breaths start to come more easily I go to the mini-fridge we keep in the office, get out a bottle of water and bring it to her. She twists off the cap and takes a sip. The shaking has stopped. I wait. She will figure out how to get to the next stage of relief. Talk would be fine. So would silence.

"Thanks, Irene," she says. Her voice is level. "Have you got a bit of time to talk?"

"I do."

"Okay," she says, "but how do I explain it to you? It's mixed up in my head, the stuff from today and the stuff from years ago that has crept up on me today. I have no idea where to start."

"What's in your head at this moment?" I ask.

"Corn," she says.

"All right," I say. "Start with corn. And let's see where that takes us."

"For me, corn means freedom," she says. "Doesn't that sound ridiculous?"

"No," I say. "Go on."

"Last night," she says, "Eric and I had Taber corn with supper—Alberta's best, maybe the world's best—and after we ate I sank my teeth into the bare cob and broke it into chunks and sucked the juice out. It's a noisy process, I know that. Just can't resist that Taber corn juice."

I don't know how corn cob sucking leads to panic, but it's Sandra's story to tell in her own way.

"Eric likes to see me enjoy my bizarre little corn ritual. He says it speaks of my joyful nature. But thirty-plus years ago, when I was in my twenties—long before Eric entered my life—I lived with a guy named Chris and he was not so charmed by my corn routine. By the way, I don't suck cob in public—you do understand that."

"Never crossed my mind you would," I say. "We've all got queer habits that we don't reveal away from home. Personally, I have a thing about keeping my navel spotless, completely clear of lint. But it's not something I take care of when I'm out on the sales floor dealing with customers."

"Right. Well, one night, Chris and I had corn for dinner—it was just the two of us, in the privacy of home—

and we had never had corn on the cob together before—and once we'd finished the—you know—conventional part of the eating, I sank my teeth into the bare cob and bit off a chunk. Then, of course, I sucked. Well, Chris blew a gasket, and before I knew what was happening, he was beating the life out of me."

"Because of your corn ritual?"

"Yeah, supposedly that was a good enough reason. Then lots of things started to set him off—me sucking on chicken bones; me overcooking pasta; me not shifting from second to third gear fast enough."

"All those were crimes punishable by beating?"

"That and more. He was always finding new reasons to get furious and physical. And he kept finding new techniques."

"Like what?"

"Humiliation. Like one Saturday afternoon, we were walking down the street together. I was depressed and not talking. He kicked my ankle.

" 'Piece of shit,' he said. 'You're a piece of shit.' And by then, I believed him.

"How many times did he blacken my eye, break my glasses, berate me for not being a perfect housekeeper? Finally I had an affair."

"Who could blame you?" I say.

"At first it was a relief to have someone treat me with kindness. But my boyfriend-on-the-side was married too, with three little kids, and I felt as guilty as sin toward his wife. So I broke it off."

"Must have been tough," I say.

"It was. And then I confessed to Chris, although I was afraid he'd beat me to death. But here's the confusing bit. He forgives me, buys me flowers, takes me to dinner. As soon as we get home he changes. Just like that. Suddenly he's in a silent rage. His face is contorted as if he's possessed. He punches me full force. Left side of the face. Eye, lower jaw, mouth. I scream, threaten to call the police.

" 'About what?' he says. 'I'm not doing anything to you.'

" 'Go to your own room now,' he says, and I say, 'I have no room, only the one we share.'

" 'You heard me. Go to your room.'

"I start heading up the stairs, thinking maybe I can reach the phone in the bedroom somehow, but he comes after me, pulls me around to face him. He pins me onto the staircase. Grabs hold of my hair and starts beating my head up and down onto a stair. I'm thinking, *This is it, I'm about to die.*"

"But you didn't die," I say. "You got through it, and you're with me now. Safe."

"I break free of him somehow, run down the stairs and out the door. I'm wearing heels but terror carries me down the street. I reach my friend Myra's house and call the police. They're good to me and they act fast."

"What happened before you came into our store today, Sandra?" I ask gently. "What's brought you back to that awful night?"

"He liked to hit me on the left side of the face. I've had surgery for a detached retina on the left eye, that eye has also bled inside, I've got a jaw disorder on the left side,

I've lost three teeth on the upper left palate."

But how does that connect to today? I'm thinking. *Patience.*

"Today at the supermarket I had a cashier. I read her name tag. Shirley. She scanned my groceries quickly, packed them efficiently and told me the total, one hundred eighty-two forty-six. Once we were done she thanked me pleasantly. She was a good cashier."

Still it is a struggle to figure out how this event could have led to Sandra's panic attack. Best to let her go on without interruption now. She'll let me know in her own time and way.

"After I left," she says, "I called the store on my cellphone and asked for the manager. Luckily, they put me through to him right away. I asked if the company had an employee assistance program and he said yes. I told him that I had had fine service from Shirley but was worried about her. The right side of her face was one big purple bruise and I had seen black and blue welts on her neck and upper chest. He said he had just gotten on shift and had not seen Shirley yet, but he would find out right away if she was receiving employee assistance and if not, he would see to it that she did. I said maybe she needed some healing time right now and he said, 'That could well be' and he told me this was his highest priority today—to make sure Shirley got support.

"My abuser liked the left side of the face; Shirley's likes the right. So what has changed since thirty-five years ago when I was assaulted?"

"Well," I say, "nowadays at least some companies have got those employee assistance programs."

"It's a step, I guess," she says.

She is breathing normally now, although she doesn't seem to realize it. You don't notice your breathing unless something goes wrong with it. Then you can't think of anything else.

We walk back onto the sales floor. Sandra has not come in just to get help catching her breath; she really does need some lingerie—control-top tights for the winter. In the past she has told me that she is prone to yeast infections so she cuts out the cotton gusset of the tights with a pair of scissors. That way she can breathe down below.

Later I meet my young friend Julie for coffee at the Bean Wave. She's wise for twenty-one—for any age, really.

"What would you do if a man started beating you up?" I ask.

"Kick him in the balls, gouge his eyes, call 911 on my cellphone and run like hell."

"Sounds as if you've planned your strategy carefully," I say.

"Every woman has to," she says.

"But why?" I ask.

"Because," Julie says, "those guys are still in business."

Tonight, I'm supposed to be winding down; that's what I've promised myself. My neck hurts from tension. I make a cup of chamomile tea and sit down with my Chatelaine magazine. I read words but their meaning doesn't register. I turn on the TV to watch the news. They lead with that New York incident. Finally I learn the full story. A twenty-year-old man has a seizure and falls on to a subway track in New York. A fifty-year-old man, Wesley Autrey, makes a split-second decision, jumps in, sees the train emerging through the tunnel, hurls the young man into a narrow drainage trough in between the rails. Then he throws his own body over the young guy's. By now the driver can see what's happening and reacts, but the emergency brake can't stop the train fast enough and it passes over them, with two inches leeway between them and the underbelly of the train. They both make it.

What drove Mr. Autrey to do what he did for that young guy? What drove Chris to do what he did to Sandra? I don't get it. They're members of the same species. My species.

Voilà

BEFORE G-18, MY LIFE was organized, which is what I need. I'm the type, I get up at six in the morning, I arrive at appointments fifteen minutes early, I sort my underwear by percentage of cotton in the blend. It's an elaborate network for protection against the world and my monsters. That's why I chose accounting. For order. My mind takes off on me, confidence fluctuates between zero and sub-zero, words get stuck between thought and utterance. But keeping scheduled and tidy helps. Structure sedates monsters. Not now though. Not since G-18.

What does G-18 do? Could she be a number-cruncher too? We've got the same taste in fashion. But then, that straight-line cut works best for our short-waisted body type, so maybe what she wears says nothing about her job, if she's got one. And anyway, all I see is the stuff she has rejected.

There's no telling when this third stage will end. It's like trying to say when a person will move to the next stage in dying and grieving. When do you go from denial to anger and then on to bargaining? Maybe the order will change. Maybe you'll die in the middle. You can't schedule your unfolding.

For a committed consignment shopper you're also on a pendulum, as you swing between necessity and pleasure. Normally, you know which end of the swing you're on as you browse through that shopful of worn threads. But now this G-18 mess has thrown the system out of balance.

First stage. I was finally done with university and training, and had just picked up my accreditation. I hung my shingle and struggled to build up my client base. With student loans to pay back, office overhead, and not much revenue, I had big cash-flow problems. Still, I had to present well, so my prospects wouldn't see me as a loser. I needed a credible business wardrobe on a pathetic budget.

That's how necessity drove me to Voilà, where they deal in quality castoffs. Classic daywear, chic casual, upscale retro. Voilà allowed me to look the part of the rising young professional and still pay the rent on my office.

With time, my business grew, until it was healthier. I wasn't going to make the Fortune 500 but I was solvent. The one part I hated was the marketing. Self-promotion is not me. For the most part, I relied on referrals.

Four years, a breast-reduction surgery, and two failed relationships after the start of my career as a Voilà regular, I entered the second stage—shopping for pleasure. Finally I could afford to buy well-made clothes brand-new, and I did some of that. But hanging out at Voilà was more fun.

Had G-18 had already surfaced? Did I fail to notice?

When the dot-com bubble burst, my business got back into trouble. Lots of my clients were in the Internet game, and their crash hit me full-force. Besides, I had believed in that high-tech sector, and made risky investments in all the wrong companies.

Meanwhile, Voilà was going through its own stages. Susie, the original owner, got fed up. She decided to buy a motorhome, drive to Arizona, and set up a new business designing headstones for a pet cemetery. She sold the store to a husband and wife who couldn't stand each other. A month after they took over, you could see they were taking their bitterness out on poor Voilà. Low inventory, chaotic merchandising. I'd walk in, there would be nobody on the sales floor or behind the counter, but you could hear the two of them bickering in the back room. Just when it seemed like Voilà would never come through, the couple decided to split up. So of course, the first thing they did, they looked to sell the store.

Enter Tanya. By the time she arrived on the scene, Voilà looked unsalvageable. I'll bet she got it for a damn good price.

Tanya's about my age I think, pushing forty. She's on her own, no kids, and I can see she wants to leave her mark. Before she bought the store, she worked for a cement contractor as an accounts receivable clerk. Not the clearest path to posterity. When her dad died and left her a nest egg, the way was clear for her to buy Voilà. She shut the place down for a week, gutted it and carried out a major reno. Did all the work on her own, she and her friend Joline who works as a finishing carpenter.

And when Voilà re-opened, Tanya never let her energy flag. She runs the place single-handed, and she is a great multitasker. She can be smiling at a customer, placing a phone order for high-density plastic bags, and reconciling a bank statement, all at the same time. Not me. At my office, it's one slogging thing at a time, with inattention and self-doubt buzzing around my head like mosquitoes. I wouldn't dare hire help. By the time I figured out what to do on my own and what to delegate, the day would be over.

What about G-18? Has she got her own business? Has she got help?

I'll tell you one advantage of being self-employed. You can get out and shop whenever you want. Not like the poor wage slaves. So what if they've got financial security, health benefits, pension plan, promotions, paid vacations? Look at the restrictions on their shopping time.

A smart consignment shopper—and I do put myself in that category, in spite of my shortcomings—a smart shopper will show up at the store on a weekday morning, early in the week, when the place is dead. Personally, I like to visit Voilà on a Monday morning as soon as they open their doors. That way, I can ease into my own work week gradually, fend off Monday blues. Plus, showing up then allows me to get acquainted with the owner and receive the best possible service. Susie used to take me into the back room and offer me items that hadn't been processed, hadn't hit the sales floor yet. Tanya won't ever do that for me though. She goes by the book.

Here's how I came into the G-18 mystery. Tanya was running a summer clearance. I came in here on a Monday morning and pulled a bunch of things to try on—sun dresses, shorts, long cotton skirts, a black shell. The items I picked could have been custom-made for me. The shorts were even good in the rise, which I am super-fussy about.

As she was writing up the bill, Tanya said, "Of course. This makes perfect sense." She explained that all the pieces I had chosen came from one consignor.

"What's her name?" I asked.

"G-18," she said.

The next time I was in, Tanya directed me right away to G-18 stock. Skirt, dress pants. Everything black, my colour. Once again, the great fit, superb cut. I bought the lot.

Seasons changed. G-18's discards took me through autumn and set me up for winter.

By the beginning of December, my one-woman company was faltering so badly I considered winding it up. But that would mean personal failure. And the prospect of conducting a job search brought on panic attacks. I decided to stick it out for another quarter, then reassess. December is a lousy month to make business decisions.

The week before Christmas, I went to Voilà and picked up a piece for the so-called festive season, a long chiffon skirt. G-18's, of course. By then I was getting curious. I asked Tanya if she knew what G-18 was planning for the holidays.

"I think she's out of town," she said.

"Where did she go?"

"I really couldn't say."

"What's her name?"

Tanya just looked at me.

I looked back and said this with my eyes: Yeah, I know. I run an accounting business. You don't disclose the identities of your clients. Same with lawyer and clients, doctor and patients. It's the confidentiality thing. The privilege thing. But let's get a grip here. We're not talking AIDS, divorce settlement, net worth. We're talking last year's dresses and tank tops.

I don't know how much of my unspoken message Tanya got. A no-nonsense obsessive is not necessarily your best people-reader.

Now, it's time for a small self-congratulatory pat. I have managed to get through Christmas again. It's always tough for me. All that socializing.

There's no point in keeping the office open between Boxing Day and New Year's. Nobody wants to do business. I don't want to venture out of my apartment. Just want to mull. How's G-18 doing? Does she get holiday blahs too? Not likely, since she can afford a winter vacation. A pricey vacation, judging by the quality of her former clothes. Probably one of those Club Med all-inclusives. What a waste. If I had that kind of money, I'd tour the great cities on foot. Take the pulse of Rome, Rio, Hong Kong. You won't find me rotting on an anonymous beach. G-18 makes hollow choices.

And what's she doing consigning her clothes anyway?

It's not as if she needs the money. She should be giving all this stuff to charity, so that women who are up against it can get the benefit. Her outfits should not be going to the likes of me. I've got an education, an apartment, a business—such as it is. I'm not in dire need; just taking advantage of G-18's greed. Does that make me complicit?

* * *

With January almost done, my business is still in the gutter. When your clients go under themselves, how are you supposed to get those word-of-mouth referrals? Too bad I never learned to do bankruptcy and insolvency work. I could be making a killing.

I place ads in the dailies and the alternative press. I can't afford to advertise, but I've got to bring in some new clients fast, or I'm gone.

A few accounts dribble in, including two start-up companies that seem to be well-financed. I get a bit of breathing space. But I also need a lift. Stamina is low. I've got seasonal affective disorder or something. I've got to impress those new clients and bring in a lot more. Time to enhance the wardrobe again. Look successful, be successful, blah blah blah. Damn G-18, she doesn't have to worry about looking better than she feels, just shops for the hell of it. Must be nice.

What *does* she do anyway, G-18, when she is not tanning on a beach or buying clothes that she later foists onto me?

I tell Tanya, strictly business wear today. She brings me

a forest green business suit, double-breasted, virgin wool. Good price. I go to the fitting room, try it on. Doesn't need so much as a hem alteration. Looks new. How many times did G-18 wear this suit before she chucked it? Once? How can she keep up her own clothing supply when she dumps her stuff so soon after she buys it?

* * *

Today I'll wear the forest green suit to work. When I do my full-length mirror check at home, I see that I chose well. This suit says authority. The woman in the suit says nothing. Fear has plucked out her tongue.

At the office, I'm thinking, what was G-18 doing while she wore this suit? I can see her sitting at an arts board meeting with a bunch of other rich women, every one of them with a thousand, fifteen hundred dollars on her back. Or maybe G-18 is running something. She's a film producer, or the manager of a hedge fund, or the CEO of a telecommunications firm. She speaks fluently; never grasps for words like I do. Her black hair is pulled back tight in a bun. The glass ceiling has shattered all over the floor of her huge office. She's got men in dark suits picking up the shards. She sits behind her massive mahogany desk issuing orders. Somehow the glass splinters have missed her desk.

But what's wrong with her breasts? Where are they? I know she has breasts. We wear the same clothes. Her blouse is too sheer. I can see through it. That's one piece I won't pick up at Voilà. Look what G-18 has done to herself. She has wound tensor bandaging around and around her breasts, flattened them, like she is acclimatizing to life without, like she is in the middle of an female-to-male sex change. How can she stand the constriction? How can she stand her own behaviour? She's yelling at the men now. The corners, she says, Don't forget to sweep the corners. I want this floor mopped after, I don't want any fragments left on this floor, not even microscopic ones. And after the wash, waxing. You get on your hands and knees and wax this floor, and then you buff it until the hardwood shines like a mirror, you hear me?

I check my watch. Five forty-two. G-18's power suit has presided over another zero day.

Where is G-18 now? Will she be at Voilà anytime soon, to update her account, collect her share of the money from the clothes I bought? Will she ask Tanya who made those purchases? Has Tanya told her about me? Am I a number too? X-24? M-67? Why did Tanya give her that bizarre name? G-18. Sounds like an economic summit. Or a jet fighter.

G-18 has taken away my taste for food. She's killed what's left of my will to work. I need to build new accounts, go to Chamber of Commerce meetings, glad-hand, suck up. I never could do that networking thing well. Now that I need it the most, I can't do it at all.

It's G-18's fault. I've got her on my head, on my back.

My business is moribund. I start a new daily routine of reading through the want ads, checking the jobs on the Internet. I post my résumé electronically on job placement websites. As I read through the want ads I'm thinking, Does G-18 work for that company? Does she own it? Maybe she will hire me on the strength of my wardrobe.

I'm going to write her a letter, and in it I am going to ask a couple of questions. Question One: Who the hell are you? Question Two: Who the hell do you think you are? Dear G-18, Do you know what it's like to walk into a coffee shop you have been in a hundred times before, and you can't place your order? You are afraid to talk to the eighteen year old behind the counter, afraid to stand in line with the young grandmother and the old stockbroker, afraid they may at any moment start talking to you.

What do you want of me, G-18? Do you want me to find a job in a big office full of people and their poison? Should I take the civil service exam, become a shut-down soul in a bureaucrat's cubicle? Or do you want me to keep my solo practice open? Why? So you can watch it die? Do you like to watch? What will you wear to the funeral? Or do you want to keep the business alive? Hurry; it's an emergency. Bring me your receipts, your invoices, your tax returns. Bring me your books. Not on a Monday, though. I'll be at Voilà, trying on clothes that you have deep-sixed.

Last stage is over. What now? How long can a stageless person survive?

G-18 forces me out to jabber with talking heads, kicks me back into the shame-shell, yanks me out again. No courtesy.

Broke now. Still, on Monday at Voilà, career wear calls.

I spot an expensive well-made blazer. What the hell—no charge for trying on. I see from the tag it is not a G-18 item. After I've got the jacket on, I raise my arms to test for fit. The back lining rips open.

Blue Thread

First letter to my mother

Mommy,

Why didn't you tell me about this stuff?

Wait, that's not how I wanted to say it. It's coming out all wrong. Too confrontational, too much shifting of blame.

Blame for what?

Time betrayed you. You were meant to become a grand old lady. Instead you were dead at fifty-nine. But you must have gone through menopause. How was it?

Nobody talked about it then. Tell me now. Please.

First conversation with my self

Mirror, mirror.

You can see the botched suicide attempt at age twenty, the seventy-two-hour spongebath of your feverish baby daughter, the crying jag when your parents said, No, you can't go to Europe with a boy, he's sure to corrupt you.

Ahead, what? Decline? Illness? Dementia? Or greater control?

In childbirth classes the instructor says, It's all about control. Keep your eyes glued on your focal point to keep control of the contraction. Control your breathing during the contraction. Rest between contractions to stay in control. The instructor visits you in the eighteenth hour of anaesthetic-free dry labour. You don't want to disappoint. You fake perfect concentration and perfect breathing for three contractions. That's it, that's it, total control, the instructor says. When she leaves, you let loose.

Now, you hit fifty, career's okay, relationship's good, no more pregnancies in the cards, no more diapers, no more first-day-of-kindergarten jitters to help your kid through.

You have learned not to take crap.

Now what?

Your period doesn't come, doesn't come, doesn't come. You figure it's for sure now, you're done. You call your friends and say, Guess what, I've arrived. Then, on Day Sixty-One, boom, you get your rag.

What kind of control is that?

Conversation with my new medicine woman

You're in choppy waters but you are a strong paddler. On the other side of this is calm.

You do have a medical degree?

Oh yes.

Why don't you sound like other doctors?

I breathe through my fingernails. I would like to move a

small herd of elephants into my bathroom. I am the emotional matrix of my family.

No wonder we connect.

Pick a card. Any card.

First conversation with my thirteen-year-old daughter

You still can't tell me to shut up, no matter how close you are to your period. You have problems with hormone levels? Me too.

Second letter to my mother

No wonder it's coming out all wrong. You never helped me get ready for this one.

Thanks to your two-year training program, I knew exactly what to do when the first period came. Look for the blue thread running down the centre of the pad. Keep the blue thread on the bottom, away from the body. Secure the ends of the pad to the clasps on the front and back of the belt. Make sure the long end of the pad is in the back.

We practised a lot before I ever bled.

When I was four years old, you prepared me for motherhood with these words: When you hold your baby, hold her close.

But we never talked about menopause.

Can we talk now, Mommy? Can you give me the language, the tips, the tools?

First conversation with my friend
Eighty-five days. You?

Twenty-three. But then, the time before, I went more than three months. I'm all over the place. Plus forgetful. The night sweats are the worst.

For me, the worst thing is feeling misunderstood.

That too.

Are you taking anything?

Evening primrose oil, ginseng, black kohosh, devil's claw. All the beneficial herbs.

Dong Quai?

You bet.

My doctor says it's unproven.

What do Western doctors know?

This one is different. A medicine woman.

Consignment store incident
I'm standing in line with the skirt I have chosen folded over my arms. The two women in line ahead of me are

about my age.

Looking straight at me, the salesperson says, Oops, your dress is on inside out.

I glance down, then head back to the changing room.

The women in line do not giggle. For that I am grateful.

Second conversation with my friend
Morris has offered to take Viagra.

What?

Once a week is all he can muster. Always on Sunday night. An hour later I'm ready for the next round. I mean, one orgasm is not necessarily enough.

Definitely not.

Well, he can't do a thing after the one time. He's too tired.

And in the morning?

Still hasn't recovered.

Does he sigh?

Thank the Goddess no, he doesn't do that.

Rolly sighs. We get up in the morning. I'm fixing coffee. He'll come up behind me and pat me on the shoulder a few times, pat-pat-pat. Then he lets out a huge, heaving sigh.

Don't those guys know you don't have to be ninety until you're ninety?

Would it help to find a younger lover?

Out of the question. How could I spend the night with someone who's never heard of Otis Redding?

Second conversation with my thirteen-year-old daughter
I like it when we get along.

Me too.

My friends' moms aren't as open with them as you are with me.

I am going to share plenty with you about the journey I'm on now. Because when it's your turn, I'd like you to have some traveller's aids on hand.

What do you mean, traveller's aids?

Language. Tools. Tips.

Second conversation with my self
It's not my mother's silence on the subject, that's not what is making it come out all wrong. It's because I am

trying to put boundaries on a work in progress.

Wouldn't it be wild to write about sex while having it? Then the sex and the writing would both come out wrong.

Still looking for the blue thread.

Borscht

"EAT THIS."

Madison stares at the bowl of borscht.

"At some point, you have to eat."

Why? To eat is pointless. But to stay seated at this table makes sense. Here she can live the simplicity of death, minus the pain of doing herself in. Here she will make no choices and therefore no mistakes. She will disengage from the daily news and the minutiae of her own life. There will be no shaken babies, no suicide bombings. She can sit here until she dies of natural causes in fifty-two years. She will leave the table only on a need-to-go basis—a bio break every three to four hours. She will let her body set its own rhythm for sleep and wakefulness. When the time comes to rest, she will set a cheek on the table. She will learn to sink into deep slumber seated and without a pillow. Occasionally, out of spite, she will stand up and circle the table again and again, then finally sit down when she least expects. The details of her existence will evaporate. She will not scoop up after the dachshund, collect air miles, check in on old Mrs. Siriopolous, shatter the glass ceiling, carry in groceries, or give birth, with or without epidural.

Well, there will have to be some eating after all. But not much.

Seventeen Teaspoons of Sugar

AND BEING AS HOW I did not draw blood when I hit her, the agency woman said everything was good and we could go home, that is the law of this state.

Molly has got this friend, Lila. It started, Lila's mother observed her, Molly not Lila, she was strutting out of their high school in a miniskirt that barely covered her caboose, which in Molly's case is like the hind end of a forty-year-old woman, she is too fat, which I have warned her about numerous times, to go easy on the cola, do you realize there are seventeen teaspoons of sugar in a coke, I tell her, no wonder you are borderline diabetic. She is also borderline many other things but that is not my point here. What I am saying is, Lila's mother observed her, which she phoned me about, saying, Do you allow Molly to dress like that? To which I respond, I do not, and furthermore, Molly wore jeans to school today. Well that is strange, she said, because I did see her with my own two eyes and if that was not a miniskirt I am a kumquat. Now Molly, when I asked her she said no, she did not wear that miniskirt but when I checked her backpack it was in there, it was about the size of a neckerchief and I do not know how she got it over her broad self at all, I am ashamed for her, mad she has done that, and also lied to me, I am so mad I smack her across the face and she runs to her room crying of course, but I am a Christian and I believe in discipline and it is my child not anybody else's, so it is my business.

Well the next thing, Molly told Lila I hit her and Lila said, Your mom cannot do that, she was illegal, you tell the guidance counsellor and your mom will get punished, not you. I am telling you, between that Lila and her mother, I have seen more troubles than I deserve this last little while. As if I did not have enough to start, between dealing with a fat lying daughter and everything else.

Well Molly goes to the guidance counsellor then and tells her that I hit her, I beat her, I don't know exactly what she says but it is not good and she twists, I am sure of that, because the guidance counsellor calls up my work at the call centre and I am called into my boss's office and I have to receive a call from the guidance counsellor right there in front of my boss, which is not going to help my career, especially since I have only been at that place a couple of months due to problems not of my making at my last job. Then I have to leave work and go see the guidance counsellor which leaves my boss even more thrilled, so you see what a heap of difficulties can descend upon you when you have an overweight fifteen year old who does not tell the truth and exaggerates.

So the guidance counsellor asks me flat out, Did you strike Molly, and I say yes, I had to, because she wore attire I do not approve of and I have always taught her modesty. And she disregarded my teaching, then she failed to level with me, so something had to be done, and I did it. So I was only doing my job as a parent.

Well to cut up a long story, the guidance counsellor made me go talk to this agency woman. Molly and I talked to her apart from each other, and then together, and the agency woman said she was going to keep an eye out for us. And I need to take a course to control my anger, she said, but also, Molly better smarten up. That is not how Molly remembers what the woman said but she is not the best listener, among her other qualities.

But meanwhile I have got the older daughter Erica, which I don't know how she came to be her sister's sister because her figure is just like that Jennifer actress from Friends, the one that her ignorant husband in real life walked out on her. That is how gorgeous she is, my Erica, and also always telling the truth, my angel. If I am sounding like I love her better than Molly excuse me, but who would you love more, that Jennifer girl or a living tub of lard with falsehoods coming out of her mouth? Well Erica, when she was eighteen I asked her, Tell me true, are you having intimate relations? Because I had a feeling, you know how a mother sometimes gets a feeling. And she told me no. But now she is twenty and she is expecting. I said, Why did you lie? And she said, I didn't at the time. Which that may be true technically but I don't believe it. Then why did you not tell me as soon as you knew, instead of that you waited five months until I saw your belly? To that she said she had not been sure, not all the evidence was in yet. Well. Even if I argued with that it would not change the facts of life in this family as we know them today.

Who did this to you, I said, and she advised me the boy's name. I'll tell you what, I phoned that boy and said, You better get yourself over here and help my girl, not to mention your future kid. Hey lady, your girl pushed herself on me, he said, I didn't even want to but she insisted, I had no choice. Listen, that baby does not care how the events came to pass, I said, it just needs a father or at the very least child support. But he hung up the phone on me so that was that.

Then my fallen angel said to me, You see how mean he is, the whole thing was not my fault. And I said, You know, it turns out you are a liar just like your fat little sister, and here I had so much trust in you.

So now the way things are left, I see the one is no better than the other, and where they learned to make up these fantasy tales I do not know, but the way things stand all I can say is, I wish I had boys instead, they must surely be less trouble.

Duck for Cover, Joan

(Fourteen years at home. But...CV prepared by a pro. Laser printed. Blue covers. No typos. New gray suit, red silk blouse, black patent pumps. Hours of research. Annual reports. Org charts. Mission statements. Marketing goals. Ready.)

MYSELF FROM HUMAN RESOURCES:
Come in, Joan.

(Firstnaming. Today's way? Cavernous room. High ceiling. Windowless. Carpet that doesn't show dirt. Three of them. Sitting at tactical intervals on one side of a boardroom table. Three bottles of cell expanding facial cream in action. Three designer labels on their backs. Three clashing scents. Three rising corporate smiles. When shall we three meet again? On the other long side, dead centre, one swivel chair. Sit, wobble. Where's my centre of gravity?)

MYSELF FROM HUMAN RESOURCES:
We are the selection panel. We will conduct a targeted interview.

(Where's the target? Duck for cover.)

MYSELF FROM HUMAN RESOURCES:
Meet my colleagues. The Department Manager. The Support Staff Supervisor. And Myself, from Human Resources.

(Human Resources. Oil and gas. Flotsam and jetsam.)

Are you prepared for the challenge of an administrative assistant position? Do you enjoy doing deadline driven, demanding, multi-faceted work which requires you to see the big picture as well as every last infinitesimal detail? Are you a control freak? A shirker? A self starter? A team player? A free spirit? Are you above making coffee? Are you now or have you ever been a member of the Bruce Springsteen Fan Club?

(I see now. The Inquisition. Rise above. Keep the faith.)

MYSELF FROM HUMAN RESOURCES:
Do you know Microsoft Word? Word Magic? Abi Word?

ME:
I know and love the Word.

MYSELF FROM HUMAN RESOURCES:
Scenario. You book a hall for nine hundred. You confirm

the booking three times. Forty-five minutes before the event you find out the hall has been double booked and you're getting bumped. What do you do?

ME:
I do what I do before every battle. I pray.

MYSELF FROM HUMAN RESOURCES:
Where do you turn for professional development?

ME:
I listen to voices.

MYSELF FROM HUMAN RESOURCES:
Voices?

ME:
The voice of the blessed Saint Michael. The voices of the blessed Saints Catherine and Margaret.

MYSELF FROM HUMAN RESOURCES:
At one time, you were a teacher's aide in a junior high school?

ME:
Yes, but the canonization came as a surprise.
(Well lubricated interrogators. Sipping with professionalism from ceramic coffee mugs. Myself From Human Resources places her cup on an off-white leather coaster.)

ME:
Please, my throat is dry. So close to the stake.

MYSELF FROM HUMAN RESOURCES:
Pardon?

ME:
Probably out of the question. But may I go for water? (Myself From Human Resources rings a bell. A woman comes in now. No intro. No designer title.)

MYSELF FROM HUMAN RESOURCES:
Bring water to the accused.

ME:
I can get it. I don't want to make another person wait on me.

MYSELF FROM HUMAN RESOURCES:
She is not waiting on you. She is waiting on us. End-stage. Do you have any last words?

ME:
Flame beyond the flame.

MYSELF FROM HUMAN RESOURCES:
We'll let you know.

ME:
Before or after the Dauphin takes the throne?

Soft Dressing

LONG-RANGE GOALS WERE NOT the problem. Felicia was clear on her goals. As soon as she could get herself out of children's wear, she wanted to either have a kid or become a makeup consultant. The problem was that she had an immediate decision to make, a life altering choice, and she was wavering wildly.

Felicia liked to make people look good. Why else would she have recommended a haircut and colour change to Frances or a nose job to Chantal? Chantal took her advice but Frances didn't. After the surgery Chantal had guys flopping all over her; now she was in a steady relationship. Meanwhile, Frances sat at home dying of loneliness.

The three of them had been friends since high school. Now, twelve years later, Frances worked as a technician in a microbiology lab, analyzing stool samples for a hospital. Chantal altered and steamed overpriced silk designer suits at a ladies' clothing boutique. And she, Felicia, had been stuck in a substandard kidswear store for the past five years, making a pittance, waiting for her life to turn around.

She hated the way customers tried to negotiate even though prices were supposed to be firm. She hated the way four-year-olds knocked over displays. She hated the way head office scrimped on quality, so that she knew as she rang in a sale that the reds would run in the first wash and the seams would rip at the playground. She hated her paltry hourly wage and she hated being treated like a non-person because she was in retail.

What made her job even bearable was the small business she ran on the side. Her mother, who lived in Nevada, manufactured T-shirts, sweatshirts, and jogging pants which were designer brand knock-offs. In fact, the average person would not even know these items were not the real thing, because every piece carried a perfect facsimile of a designer logo on it.

Felicia took orders and distributed her mother's goods from the stockroom of the children's clothing store. She knew that what she was doing was not strictly legal, but the store manager didn't seem to mind and Felicia knew she was helping her mother, not to mention herself—her mother gave her a generous cut. Besides, her customers appreciated the service. The ones who came in for this product were much nicer to her than the ones she dealt with on the sales floor of the store. Even in the case of overlapping business, a person buying a quasi-designer adult T-shirt behaved much more respectfully than the same person buying a toddler's snowsuit.

Chantal had gone and gotten herself knocked up. Of course she was going ahead with the pregnancy; she had always dreamed of being a mom. Felicia was annoyed—she wanted to be the first in the group to have a baby. But circumstances had gotten in her way. Since the age of eighteen, she had gone through one lousy boyfriend after another. Evan did hard drugs, Damon chased teenaged girls, John mooched money, Paul obsessed over his old girlfriend. Then there were the mothering problems. Raj mothered her, Justin wanted her to mother him, Kyle couldn't separate from his mother.

And they all wanted sex all the time.

Not that Felicia was against sex. A bit of sex now and then was fine. It just was not what drove her. Frances was like her that way. But Frances wanted a lot of conversation with a man; Felicia preferred to talk to her women friends. Chantal was the one the other two called "normal." The first thing Chantal noticed about any guy was the shape of his bum.

Much as she loved Frances and Chantal, there was a time of day when Felicia could not see or even talk to them. That time was the evening. It was her refuelling time. She had to spend it tranquilly at home reading, listening to music, just being. At the same time, she was not happy spending the evening entirely alone. Prolonged solitude caused her to become too introspective and self-critical. She had battled depression on and off since childhood. She felt she could keep it at bay better in the presence of a suitable mate. But as simple as her needs were, she worried that she would never meet the right man—one who would spend the evenings quietly with her—one who would be fully there, to participate with her in the experience of being.

When she first met Conner she thought she had found the right man. Conner was not a big talker. His sexual demands were moderate. He impressed her with his quiet charm, his ability to be fully there. A month after they started going out, she invited him to move in with her.

But once they began living together, Conner changed. His quietness took on an ominous quality. He became sullen. He had big wordless mood swings. He started doing strange things—staring at her, not flushing the toilet, drinking too much. His silent turmoil filled up all the space in the apartment. Felicia asked him to leave. He went to stay with his sister.

But Felicia missed the male companionship in the evenings, she became sad and inward-looking again, and when Conner asked to come back she put up no resistance. On his return, Conner was calm again. But within a couple of months, he reverted to the brooding, the passive aggression. She sent him away to his sister, and in two weeks he returned. Things went well again until the next episode.

They had gone on this way for four years now—together, apart, together, apart. Last year, they had considered marriage just to get out of the exhausting on-again off-again cycle. However, Felicia said, she would not go ahead with a marriage until she could be absolutely sure of stability.

Six weeks ago, without explanation, Conner had arranged for the post office to forward all his mail to his sister's house. He started driving over to the sister's place frequently, supposedly just to pick up the mail, and sometimes he wouldn't be back at the apartment for days at a time.

Felicia considered the possibilities. Was Conner sick of the relationship? Was he seeing someone else? In other words, was he gearing up to leave her? She could not allow that to happen. She and Frances and Chantal had had many discussions on this subject over the years and had settled on the protocol: dump him before he dumps you.

Because she and Conner had gone through the motions so many times before, Felicia was confident that she could carry out a quick, clean break-up when she next saw him. Given his recent pattern, that should be within the next few days.

But now that the Conner issue was settled, at least in her mind, she had that big decision to make. If she decided against, the cost would be high—heavy depression. If she decided for, she could not predict the outcome; she might wind up paying the highest price—humiliation.

The responsibility of deciding had been weighing heavily on Felicia, even before she had conclusively settled on dumping Conner. She had been acting peculiar at work, warning customers against the faulty zippers, the poorly finished buttonholes, the inevitable shrinkage of the fabrics. In the interests of self-preservation, she made these disclosures when she was the only staff member on the floor. But her falling sales turned into a steady pattern, and the manager gave her a formal reprimand. She would need to improve her productivity right away; her job was on the line. But by now Felicia was so worried about her impending decision that she hardly cared about the job.

She called her mother and asked her not to send any new quasi-designer product for the time being. She did not want to deal with the extra responsibility while contemplating her decision.

Frances, who had a fixation on animals, invited her to a dog show. Felicia said she was working that day and couldn't go. In fact it was her day off and she had no plans.

Chantal wanted to get together to talk about her childbirth options. She was tempted to go the alternative route—midwives, home births, and so on—but she was afraid something might go wrong. Felicia said a sinus infection was getting the best of her and she could not meet to discuss Chantal's stuff.

Nor could she allow Frances and Chantal to know about her own stuff. Tempted as she was to share her burden with them, she had to bear it alone. The problem was, what if they were to counsel her to make the wrong choice? Her friendships with them could be jeopardized. She couldn't take that risk.

Finally Felicia could no longer bear the pressure of indecision. She gave herself a deadline of Tuesday morning. Today was Friday. Tuesday was her next day off so she could do what she had to that day if the answer was yes. She had looked at it from every angle and she was leaning heavily toward yes.

Conner came home Monday night. She didn't give him a chance to say anything. She asked him to pack, said it was final. They both knew the script; he was out in an hour. This time, though, Felicia called the landlord and arranged to get the locks changed. The whole business was strictly transactional for her. She felt no different than she did when she rang in a sale.

On Tuesday morning after the locksmith had come and gone, she kept her commitment to herself and made her decision. She was going for yes.

She checked the yellow pages to find out where to go. Then she phoned the transit company to find out how to get there. The place was deep in the suburbs. Felicia had always lived and worked downtown. She detested the outskirts; she went there only when necessary. Frances had dragged her to a couple of cat shows in an arena in the boondocks; on the drive down Felicia was sickened by the sterility of the neighbourhood.

But now she had no choice. She certainly was not going to do this particular business any place that was within her regular territory.

Of the three friends, Frances was the only one who drove. Felicia was tempted to ask her for a lift, but of course she couldn't. First of all, Frances would be busy at the lab counting E. coli bugs. In any case, how would

Felicia explain why she needed the ride? Where would she have Frances drop her off? What would Frances do while she waited for Felicia to finish her business—count picket fences? It would be better to put up with slow, circuitous routes and long waits at godforsaken suburban bus stops. She would remember to take along a book.

Felicia prepared carefully before leaving. It was, of course, always important to look good. But today she needed to look good in precisely the right way. She had to be approachable yet businesslike in her appearance. Relaxed yet alert. Discreet yet savvy. Soft dressing was the obvious answer. She settled on her mid-calf length floral skirt, slingback heels, and navy crewnecked tunic sweater. She rejected textured and silky options in favour of simple flesh coloured pantyhose. She wore her hair up and kept the makeup subtle.

She forgot her book. The trek was long and irritating. Finally she arrived at the correct stop and got off the bus, which was right in front of her destination. But she could not bring herself to walk in.

She was standing, immobilized, at one end of a strip mall. Her new plan was to walk to the other end and collect herself. Four stores and twenty-five paces later, the plan had been executed. Still, she could not go back where she wanted to be.

She crossed the street and walked around a block filled with bungalows, two-car driveways, heavily fertilized lawns. Boredom drove her back to her objective. She returned to the strip mall and walked into a shop.

The woman at the back looked normal enough. Dress pants, loose-fitting short sleeved blouse, heart shaped silver pendant. She was greying at the temples. Mid-fifties, Felicia figured. Could shave off five to seven years with a professional makeover, daily facial exercises and a deep auburn semi-permanent hair rinse.

"Lovely day," the woman said, as though the situation were normal.

Felicia could not bring herself to play the small talk game. "I need—I'm looking for an inflatable doll," she said.

"Male or female?"

"Male."

"Any preferences?"

After a moment of hesitation, Felicia said, "Tall."

"I'll bring you some options," the woman said. Then she disappeared into the stock room.

Felicia was not sure she wanted options.

When the woman came back she had three boxes with her, each of them about the size of a dictionary. "I'm afraid this is all I can offer you in males," she said. "We have a much wider selection in females." Felicia looked at the first box. On the front was a picture of an expressionless stud in leopardskin jockey shorts.

"Let me tell you about the features," the woman said.

"That's okay," Felicia said.

She read the writing on the box.

ERIC YOUR MAN
• DETAILED MANNEQUIN HEAD
• ROOMY MOUTH
• TWO LOVE ENTRYWAYS
• HOLDS 225 POUNDS
• DETACHABLE NINE INCH VIBRATING DONG
Takes 2 AA batteries. Batteries not included.

"I'll—how much is it?"

"This one is two forty," the woman said.

"Two hundred and forty dollars?" Felicia said. "Ouch."

"Well, it's imported," the woman said.

"I see. Okay. I'll take it."

"Can I offer you the repair kit? It's a little bit extra but we recommend it."

"I don't...not today, thanks. I'll take my chances."

Felicia got out her credit card. The woman put through the sale. Then she reached down and pulled up an unmarked brown paper bag. The appearance of this stereotype gave Felicia her first pleasant moment in the store. She pictured a large bright orange plastic handled bag with SEX TOY emblazoned on it in huge purple letters.

While the woman wrapped, Felicia glanced at the display case next to the cash desk. Dildos. Waterproof vibrators. Latex extensions. The Double Header. Failing a manufacturing defect in the doll she had just bought, she doubted that she would be back.

When she got home she took the doll out of the bag.

The detachable penis turned out to be a separate piece. Felicia let it lie in the box. The doll would not be needing it today. She blew the doll up, dressed him in his leopardskin jockey shorts. Then she went to work with a measuring tape, writing down in a pocket notebook the numbers she needed.

She thought about what fun it would be to call Frances and Chantal to carry out the next step. But for the second time that day, she had to make a critical shopping trip alone. She went to Borman's Men's Wear and picked up two pairs of trousers, two golf shirts, two sweaters. She was careful to choose mix and match separates so that she would not have to look at the same one or two outfits day after day. As an afterthought, she picked up a pair of socks. Then she headed off to the shoe store. Would dress shoes fit over latex? She could hardly ask the salesman. She chose sneakers, which were cheaper and more flexible. She did not have a good mental picture of the doll's feet, but size eleven was her best estimate. Conner wore a size eleven and the doll was about his height. If the shoes were too small she could always squish the feet a tad to make them fit.

Back at the apartment, she ironed the outfits and dressed the doll. She hung up the extra clothing in her closet. She sat the doll up in a living room chair, crossed his right knee over his left. She pulled a magazine off the coffee table, put it in his hands, and adjusted him into a reading position.

She spent the rest of the afternoon and the whole evening reading magazines and listening to music. She neither denied the doll's presence nor dwelled on it. He was just there with her. Fully there.

Cast Clinic

I'M A COTTAGE INDUSTRY," the guy next to me says. "I keep a lot of people working. Orthopedic surgeons. Neurologists. Physios. X-ray techies. Not to mention the alternative medicine people."

The corridor we sit in, lined with straight-backed chairs, fills up fast with the injured and the maimed. Casts, slings, linen, over-the-cast slippers with white rubber soles and beige velcro straps. Wheelchairs and crutches. Microcosm of a war zone infirmary.

"It's the knee," the guy next to me says. "Ongoing problems for fifteen years, since my high school basketball days. Last thing they did, they thought it would cure me for good—total knee replacement. Only problem, it didn't work."

Sign on the cast room wall reads, "Support an orthopedic surgeon. Ride a motorcycle."

Small room. Doctor moves constantly from first bed to x-ray display wall to second bed. Nurse saws open plaster casts, offering lightweight fiberglass replacements in hot pink, teal blue, deep purple. Nurse swabs skin that hasn't seen the light of day for weeks. We, the wounded in the corridor, we see and hear the cast room action through the open door.

"Will you have a look at that bruise?" the guy next to me says, as the nurse breaks open a knee-to-ankle cast in first bed. "Must have taken quite a blow."

Rotation time. Second bed is mine now. As Nurse saws off my cast, a diminutive ninety-year-old woman makes her way carefully into first bed. Shriveled, pinched. Shrinks a little more with every wash, perhaps. Huge plaster cast covering her right arm, wrist to shoulder. Multiple fractures? Osteoporosis taking its toll? Her frame, too tiny even for the narrow bed.

Doctor returns from the x-ray display wall and stands by the old woman's bed.

"How are you doing?" he asks.

"Without," she says in disgust. "Six years now."

Joseph

SO IF YOU KNOW his name, doesn't that tell you something? Doreen says.

Maybe I shouldn't have let her know that the cat has communicated his name to me. She's turned that into a selling point. She's nothing if not persistent, my friend Doreen Lockhart.

But I won't rush this. There's so much at stake.

You can see, just to look at the boy, he's getting on, and he's been through the wringer. I wonder how the SPCA does their age estimates. I read the tag of his cage again. *Adult male, domestic s/h, approx. 8–9 yrs.* Skinny, wasting. Who knows if I could ever get him back into shape? The coat is ragged, but what a warm colour. I've always had a weakness for marmalade toms. I read somewhere that the first cats ever in the world—the ones all the others descended from—they were orange, like this beautiful boy.

It's a good six months Doreen has been working on me to come down here and look over the animals waiting for adoption. God knows she's had enough opportunities to talk about it. We talk on the phone or get together at some point just about every day. Sure, I'm busy selling lingerie and managing Marjorie's Lingerie, even though I don't need or want the title "manager." But I can make time for Doreen. Why else were we given time?

My orange friend Joseph looks me over pretty carefully. Even when a cat is being sociable, he lets you know he is a lot smarter than you are. He likes me though. Sticks his head between the bars and nuzzles against my hand. Throws me thoughts.

I tell Doreen, I just don't know about living with other species. It's because of Percy. I treated that budgie like a two-ounce prince. I was only twelve, my mother helped me get him set up. We bought him a huge cage and lots of toys, state-of-the-art treadmill, the works. But he got sick anyway, moulted like crazy, pooped so much I couldn't keep up with the cleaning. Held on to some feathers on his wings and body, but on his head he went completely bald. One day I get home from school and find him delirious, running around in circles. I panic and put the blue cloth cover on the cage. I've got to handle this alone, my mother is at work. An hour later, I check back. No sound comes from the cage. I stand there for a long time. Finally pull the cover off. Percy lies on the floor of his cage in a tiny tight mass, feet curled under. My first look at rigor mortis.

Doreen says, You are no longer a child, and this cat is not a budgie.

But still. Think of the things cats can get. Distemper. Feline AIDS. Crystals in the urinary tract, kidney failure, cancer.

You'll make sure he has his yearly check-up and shots,

she says. Once you get him home and settled, he'll be fine.

Joseph sticks his wild rose nose out between the bars of his cage again. This time he sneezes.

See? I say.

Joseph senses his days may be numbered. I know that, the same way I know his name. You click with a cat, you realize telepathy is real.

He walks to the litter box in his cage and I watch him lift his leg to pee and I'm thinking, Ooh, isn't that adorable? Then I tell myself, whoa, let's stand back and get a little perspective here.

I need a couple of days to think, I say. We're talking about a big commitment.

This cat is not looking to get married, Doreen says.

All the next day at work, I have Joseph kicking around different parts of my head.

Two days after our first trip to the SPCA, I tell Doreen I've made my choice. We drive back down there to pick up Joseph.

When we get to the adoption area, I walk straight to his cage. A long-haired Persian sits in it, nursing her kittens.

I check all the other cages. No Joseph.

Then I know. I just know.

Maybe not, Doreen says. Maybe he's been adopted. Maybe he's getting de-wormed. We'll ask at the desk.

No, I say, let's leave now.

On the ride back I'm thinking, did he tell the vet his name?

Briefing Notes

WHEN I WAS BORN they were still putting silver nitrate into the corners of every new baby's eyes for prevention, in case the mother had syphilis. Well, with me, they missed, and my left eye got burned and swelled up like a newly manufactured golf ball. That's how it goes for me.

Take yesterday. Like I told Jasper, it wasn't my fault I arrived at the office a little late. It's because I had to wash the bandage stockings, which I was wearing after the varicose veins operation. After the surgery Jasper said, "How come you have this problem at thirty-seven? Have you secretly had a baby or what?" Well, there's no abandoned infants stashed in my past. It started with a predisposition, the doctors told me. Some kids have it in them to become musical virtuosos or master architects, if they just get the right opportunities. I had it in me to be a proud bearer of varicose veins, if life would only give me a chance. Last year I got my big break. It was a bike accident, a wipeout. The trauma made those varicose veins blossom with a passion.

I need to have a series of operations. The veins the doctors worked on this time are on the right side in the groin area. Dealing with the thick rubber bandage stockings is a major undertaking. On what Jasper pays me, I could only afford to buy one set of the stockings. I need to wash them every morning for five days after surgery, then dry them off with a blow-dryer, but just a bit at a time so they don't melt. I've got to keep the right leg higher than my heart while the bandages are off; otherwise, blood clots can reach the heart or brain. Then there's the hassle of getting the bandages back on. The fit is skin-tight and I've got to do the whole job with one leg up like a chorus dancer frozen in position. The phone is in the kitchen and I couldn't get there easily yesterday morning while going through those contortions, so I didn't phone the office until I was re-bandaged.

All of which I explained to Jasper, and he rolled his eyes and said, "Next time, call first, okay, Seema? And spare me the details."

I thought employers were supposed to be happy when workers shared information about their lives.

"Just get it done," Jasper always says. "I don't care what you have to do," he says, "just get it done." Meaning what? Meaning lie, cheat, and steal if you must, as long as you get it done? Don't be such a literalist, I tell myself, how much room is there for white collar crime when you're a secretary receptionist?

My older sister Loretta says she doesn't know why Jasper keeps me on, what with all my accidents and lates and absences. I'm too much of a professional to tell her that I clean up all of Jasper's spelling mistakes. He's a good real estate agent but he can't write worth beans. Plus my photographic memory comes in handy for him. It's a gift I discovered when I was ten years old, laid up for weeks with my leg in traction after a toboggan accident. I would read constantly to make the time pass. I made up a game—reading a page, then closing my eyes and reciting the words. It was easy. I could recreate all the pictures in my mind's eye too. And today, for Jasper, I can close my eyes and recite whole clauses of commercial leases.

I probably should have skipped my conversational French class at the university last night. Just four days post-surgery—that was pushing it. The most embarrassing part of going out in public is the bulge of the stockings in the crotch. It's especially noticeable when I'm sitting. Norman took his usual place next to me for the lesson. Then, during the break, he said, "Seema, that bulge is something else. You look like you're at half mast."

Usually I don't let guys get away with comments like that, but this is Norman. We've been friends since we were eighteen. My sister can't believe Norman and I can do so many things together and not be lovers. "Have you ever heard of friendship?" I ask her. She purses her lips. Apparently not.

Sure, sometimes Norman tries my patience. Like the time he invited fifteen people to a dinner party, and did nothing until the day of the event, and couldn't cope, and I wound up doing almost all the cooking and cleaning. Or like the time he partied and got too hammered to type up a term paper that was due the next day, so he talked me into doing it.

But then there are the other times. When Jasper's on my case or when I'm having boyfriend problems, Norman has great listening ears.

He's taking the French class because, he says, our instructor Anne Marie is a normal person giving an extension course, not a self-important academic. Norman is disenchanted with his art professors. After scrimping and saving as a waiter for years so he can go to university, and maybe eventually become a museum curator, he put all his money into a fine arts program which is turning out to be a big disappointment. "I can't breathe in those classes," he says. "The profs are so high on themselves they should check into a detox centre."

Sometimes I'll sit in Norman's living room and look at the pictures in his textbooks. My favourite one is a photograph of a statue in a text on art of the ancient world. There are writeups with the pictures so you can figure out what's going on. This statue takes you back to the last days of the war between Greece and Troy. Laocoon, a Trojan priest of noble blood, has warned his countrymen not to accept the Greeks' gift of a wooden horse. He says it's a trap. He has even tossed his spear right into the horse's flank. Laocoon's behaviour has enraged Apollo. And when you make a Greek god mad, you're in trouble. To punish Laocoon, Apollo sends two huge snakes up from the ocean to destroy him and his two young sons. The statue shows Laocoon and the little boys in the hour of their agony, entangled by the serpents.

I've gone back to the picture of that statue many times. I don't know why it draws me so.

Today, Norman calls me at work and says he has a final exam tonight and he's come down with the flu.

"So what are you going to do?" I ask. "Can you write it sick?"

"Not in the shape I'm in today," he says. "Both ends unstable, if you know what I mean."

"Can you get it deferred?" I ask.

"Not without running the bureaucratic gauntlet," he says. "I haven't got the patience."

"Oh no," I say, "then you'll get an Incomplete. Or you'll flunk."

"Not if you'll sit the exam for me," he says.

"Excuse me," I say. "You think you're the first to think up this scam? Ever heard of Teddy Kennedy? In law school he hired someone to write an exam for him and surprise, surprise, he got caught. I have a problem with this proposal of yours. A few problems."

"I'm listening," he says. Like I say, Norman will always hear you out.

I give him the two most obvious objections. It's cheating, and I don't know much about art history.

"I'll give you briefing notes over the phone," he says. "And it won't be cheating because you'll just be writing down what I told you. Think of it as a short-term secretarial gig."

That's another strength of Norman's—creativity.

I agree to his cockamamie scheme. Why? Why do I do anything for Norman? My sister says I own too many of his problems.

The briefing notes don't help much. We're talking about a twenty minute telephone conversation over my coffee break. Norman gives me the history of the world in twenty-five words or less. He tells me his student ID number, which I am to write, along with his name, on the cover of the exam booklet. He says the prof has promised an "Oxford style" exam—a choice of twelve open-ended questions. You take your pick and answer the one question for the whole two hours.

My anxiety is building so I decide to pour some tension off with a mini-workout at lunch hour—nothing too strenuous, what with the bandages and sore groin. Jasper sees me leave the office with my gym bag and says, "Don't forget to shower."

Well, you know how it is—your day never goes the way you planned it. At the gym, a guy is just coming off a treadmill as I walk by. We're both a little distracted and he smashes into me and down I go. When I get up, I can't move my neck much and there's a burning sensation down through the left shoulder and arm.

So instead of returning to work in the afternoon, I head for the hospital. The admitting clerk at Emergency says, "Hi, Seema. What now?" Two hours later, I walk out wearing a neck brace.

Do I go home and pop a couple of codeine pills like a sane person? Do I call Norman and tell him his health is a lot better than mine at this point, and he can write his own wretched exam?

I return to the office and stay late to make up for the two hours I missed. Then I pick up a bag of potato chips at the candy stand on the main floor of our office tower, and munch on the bus ride over to the university and call it supper. It's a twenty minute ride. I've brought my English translation of The Aeneid to read en route. That statue of Laocoon has got me interested in learning more about the ancients. I meet Laocoon again, and Virgil takes me to the death scene. The snakes envelop me, crush me. My priestly headband becomes saturated with blood which trickles down my forehead and into my eyes.

I become aware of rustling around me and look up. Here's my stop. Students are hoisting backpacks onto their shoulders and stepping off the bus. I follow them, and walk across campus to the Arts Building, and wonder what the hell I think I'm doing.

Thank heavens it's a big class, about three hundred students, which makes it easy not to be noticed. I pull out my student ID card, which I've got because of my night classes. The idea is to show the proctor the card, which has my photograph on it, and write Norman's name and ID number on the exam booklet. Very clever—only I know it's been done many times before.

The proctor is about my age—a grad student, no doubt. Right away I feel sorry for him. It's a while since I've seen anyone look so weary, so defeated. I figure he's been working on his thesis about nine years. The poor guy has chronic institutional fatigue.

He just glances at the ID card and calls it a day.

Does this mean I'm home? Not so fast. There's still the exam to deal with. I pencil in Norman's ID number on the front page of the exam booklet. But I don't fill in his name. Not yet.

I look at the Oxford-style questions.

1. Comment on the great advance made in civilization in the twelfth and thirteenth centuries by a sudden consciousness of feminine qualities.

2. Discuss the discovery of the individual in early fifteenth century Florence, and how this discovery was reflected in art.

3. Reflect on how the Romantic movement added awareness of the sublime to European art.

I know nothing about this stuff. Norman's briefing notes didn't cover any of it. My neck hurts and my groin is throbbing. I want to get out of here. Now.

I force myself to keep reading the questions.

11. Comment on how sympathy for the vanquished finds its way into Greek art.

Bingo.

I close my eyes. It's all there—the father in the middle, with a young son on either side of him. Snakes wrap around the younger boy's back and left arm, cover the father's right thigh, circle his left calf and twist over the limbs of the older boy. The sons instinctively look up to the father for help. Laocoon has his mouth open, in cries of pain, but also, I think, in an effort to speak. He wants to comfort his sons even in the midst of their torture and his own. He wants to tell them it will soon be over.

I don't know what I'm writing. Words spill onto the page of the exam booklet. Laocoon suffers. For what? For fighting deception. I close my eyes and bring up some stuff from the Ancient Art book, paraphrase it and throw it in for good measure. My pen continues to move on the page. I find myself referring to texts I've never read and works of art I've never seen. I'm thinking, this is like the automatic writing that I read about once in a book on psychic phenomena. The possessed person just writes, barely consciously, and all the while thinking about something else. Which is what I'm doing. I'm thinking about going to see Norman's mother in hospital, and sitting with her, and telling her Norman was in Toronto when he really was home. All because he convinced me he couldn't bear to be around illness. I'm thinking about the compliments Norman accepted at that dinner party for "his" cooking. I'm thinking. *From Ionic to Corinthian*, I'm writing—a reference to a treatise on Greek pillars. Wonder what that's all about.

My hand stops moving.

I change three digits on the ID number on the exam booklet cover. Then I hand the booklet in and walk out of the room.

Modern Fit

I WAS SPEECHLESS WHEN Frank phoned yesterday and told me we were about to start selling men's product at Marjorie's Lingerie. Usually he doesn't make many plans for our little store. He throws himself into bigger ventures—his investments and whatnot. He's vague about what he does. You find that sometimes with businessmen. But what do I know about the world of high finance?

I'm sure the business part of Frank would have sold the store long ago, but the son part of him stopped that from happening. He had such respect for his mother Marjorie, who started it up and made a go of it. Today, for Frank, the store is Marjorie's last living organ. I know what that's like. I hung on to my dead husband Henry's fishing equipment for how many years. Organs of the dead can be made out of anything and take their nourishment from the heads of the surviving loved ones.

Frank runs his affairs out of his downtown office. As far as Marjorie's Lingerie goes, he counts on me, just like his mom did. Thirty-two years now I've been handling the day-to-day at the store. I've got two best friends. One is Doreen Lockhart. The other is Marjorie's Lingerie.

You can't combine women's and men's underwear in one small store, can you? My gut says it's nuts. But Frank, once he's decided on something, it's tough to turn him around. So instead of giving him negatives right away, I just mm-hmmed my way to the end of the conversation. Before I could help the store out, I needed to understand what he was talking about. Doreen keeps telling me knowledge is power, which is why she takes one continuing education course after another. Frank will listen to an educated argument. He's headstrong, not stupid.

So on my day off, I head downtown to get educated. The classroom is Stenger's, my favourite department store. Of course I am tempted by the women's wear, but a professional concentrates on her job. On the upper level I reach my destination, men's underwear. I've got to get on with my purpose right away or I am bound to chicken out and leave. At heart, I'm a prude. There are some men shopping up here and they make me nervous. I try to look as if I have a right to be here. I am in the market for trunks. I need them for my Henry. Of course, he's been dead for twenty years and I never did buy his underwear for him, so it's not easy playing the part. But I need to stay here long enough to learn something about the product.

I can see there are lots of style choices. Hip brief, cycle short, two-button boxer with mid-thigh coverage. Midway and no-fly briefs. Low rise, modern fit. The photographs on the packages tell me the meaning of modern fit: tight. Another kind of fit is called comfortable. They are asking men to decide between being comfortable and being modern. Is this a secret of the men's side of the business? Personally, I've always told my customers, Don't choose between style and comfort. It's possible to have both in one undergarment. Not for men, I guess.

Even though I have been working with lingerie for more than half my life, the photographs on this packaging embarrass me.

Back at work the next day, I try to picture those boxes of men's product on our shelves. They don't belong.

A few days later Frank and I meet at his office for our quarterly review. At these meetings we go over the books and set new sales targets. On this day I can see that he's going through something. That furrow down the centre of his forehead is dug in so deep it splits his face in half. The lines at the corners of his mouth extend halfway down his chin, as though he were a talking puppet.

As soon as I sit down, he starts going over the numbers with me. After we are done, he says, We'll start bringing in the men's product in about six weeks.

I don't say much. I'm still not ready to talk. On my walk back, I think about how it was when I started at Marjorie's Lingerie. Frank was thirteen then. I saw him suffer with teasing because of teenaged acne. Later I saw him quit university, return and quit again. I watched him fall into two bad marriages and crawl out of them. I know when it's a bad time to talk to Frank.

Still, I worry. Personal talks rise up naturally at Marjorie's Lingerie. If we were to change the place to the way Frank wants it, would those talks happen any more? Would a man in a fitting room strike up a conversation with the woman in the next fitting room about his prostate cancer?

I know now what I need to discuss with Frank. Not possible drops in sales, not loss of market share or any of those other things he likes to discuss. I need to tell him that if he goes ahead with this notion of his, he will be ripping the heart out of Marjorie's Lingerie.

When I get the nerve up to phone him, Frank sounds chipper.

I want to talk to you about your plan for the store, I say. I have finally gathered my thoughts on the subject.

No need, he says, I listened to you at our quarterly meeting. As soon as you left my office, I cancelled the orders for men's product.

I walk home along my familiar route, which is usually a comfort, but my thoughts put me on edge. Sometimes I need to get myself good and uncomfortable; it's either that or run. What throws me now is thinking about the two Franks, the one I have constructed inside my head for thirty-two years and the one who can read me.

Cash Root

JOE WAS THE LAST to order. "I'll have the brains," he said.

What?

I waited for the server to leave.

"Am I hallucinating, or did you just order brains?" I asked.

"Yeah. Why?"

"You eat brains?"

"I read that brain fritters are scrumptious. They're not for everyone, though," Doreen said. For a girl of sixteen, she had a lot of peacemaker in her. Even today, in her sixties, she will sometimes haul out odd facts to drive away tension. She has always been a big reader—not just magazines, like me, but lots of books too—and that habit of hers has come in handy a lot over the years.

I was confused about how Doreen's plan was unfolding. Why had Sheldon taken us to a place where they served brains? I thought for sure that we'd be going to the most popular kosher restaurant in Montreal, Anna's, which *Weekend Magazine* had called one of Canada's ten leading eateries of 1964, because of its great food and inviting informality. Had Anna's lost its good name in only one year? My mother and I didn't eat out much, and when we did, it was usually in the cafeteria of Woolworth's, our favourite five-and-dime store. We weren't Jewish; I was no expert on kosher dining in Montreal. Still, I hadn't expected Sheldon to take us to this chi-chi, non-kosher place on Ste. Catherine Street, with grey matter on the menu.

"Organs can't be kosher," I said to myself, but out loud.

Sheldon thought I was talking to the world. "My mother sometimes makes pickled tongue," he said.

"A tongue is not an organ," I said.

"Let's not have a debate," Doreen said, moving one muscle on either side of her mouth to create a tiny smile. "Let's just have a swell time."

I realized I'd better shut up. Doreen had been on edge all evening, and as her best friend, it was my job to help her feel okay. That was why I had agreed to be part of her plan in the first place. I was dying to get her alone for a couple of minutes, but our dates were both nice boys, and I didn't want to offend them by signalling to Doreen or whispering in her ear. Even back in those days, whispers offended me. People don't hear each other properly anyway when they are whispering. The other people in the room always think they are being talked about, and often they're right. If Doreen and I were going to talk about Sheldon and Joe, I knew we shouldn't do it under our breath. We should do it in the privacy of the women's washroom.

As soon as the food arrived, Sheldon attacked his

chicken salad.

I couldn't help myself. "You keep kosher, right, Sheldon?" I asked.

"Yeah, I come from a kosher home."

"Well, to be kosher, doesn't the chicken have to be killed by a special guy?"

"Right you are. That's the shoichet, the ritual slaughterer. It's part of Kashruth."

"Cash root? What's that?"

"The rules on keeping kosher. You sure know a lot about this stuff, for a girl who's not Jewish."

Know a lot, my foot. He was just trying to distract me with a compliment, so I'd stop talking chicken.

"So this is not a kosher restaurant, and your salad has bits of meat in it, from a chicken that was not killed by the special guy. How can you say you keep kosher?"

"What do you mean? I do keep kosher."

"But…"

"Oh yeah, I see what's bugging you, Relax, Irene. There's no problem."

"Why not?"

"Think about it. How much chicken do you think they put in a chicken salad?"

Doreen's eyes had been darting from Sheldon to me and back. I could see that she was afraid we'd butt heads. Not a chance. I was only curious, and Sheldon had his loopy argument worked out. I didn't care what he ate; I only want to follow his thinking.

Doreen stirred her mushroom soup, never lifting the

spoon to her mouth.

I started in on my Waldorf salad. I had always loved the taste of walnuts, apples, and mayonnaise mixed together, and I was savouring my first bites, when I noticed what was sitting on Joe's plate: steamed carrot coins, roasted baby potatoes, a sprig of parsley and a blob full of folds and deep furrows. The blob was covered in a yellow sauce, maybe some kind of mustard concoction.

"How's…how are they?" I asked.

"They're okay," he says. "Not as good as my mother's brains."

"Come again?"

"My mother cooks brains. I watch her."

"Why?"

"Because I'm going to study to be a chef."

"Does she fix them like those—like the ones you've got on your plate?"

"She's got more style," Joe says. "She cuts the brains up into cubes, all the same size. She eyeballs the brains to figure out where to cut and makes a batter out of flour and beer. Then she dips the brains in the batter and deep fries them."

"Your mother serves you beer? When can I come over?" Sheldon said.

"It's different when it's heated up in food. The alcohol evaporates."

"Darn."

"Are brains kosher?" I asked.

"I have no idea," Joe said. "My family, we're not religious, we don't keep kosher, so we don't care. Sheldon, what do you say? Are brains kosher?"

"I don't know. If the animal is trayf anyway, non-kosher, like a pig or a snail, I suppose every part would be trayf. Shinbone, brain, the works."

I lost track of the conversation for a couple of minutes, as I imagined my brain being removed from my skull, cut up, and tossed into a bowlful of perfect cubes. I knew it wouldn't be painful; the year before, in grade ten biology, we had learned that there was no feeling in the brain. Still, I didn't like the idea of plain old cubes. A bunch of random shapes would make more sense. After all, the brain was where the creative juices flowed from.

Doreen started crying. What had happened? Had she read my sick mind? Or had one of the boys said something that hurt her feelings? She's such a tender soul, so easily damaged. Even then, I worried about her all the time. She ran for the women's washroom and I dashed after her. This was not the best way for us to get our private time.

Once we were in there, we locked into a hug and she got out some good sobs. Then, she rinsed her face out in one of the sinks, wiped it off with a paper towel, and reapplied her pink pearl lipstick.

"I shouldn't have pushed you into this double date, Irene," she said.

"Why not? Joe seems like an okay guy, for a cannibal. What's bugging you?"

"Our plan isn't going to work out."

"*Your* plan. I'm just along for the ride. But, so what if it bombs? At least we can have fun tonight."

I hadn't had much belief in Doreen's plan in the first place, but she had been determined to go ahead with it, and for me, friendship trumped logic. In that way, I'm the same today, forty-six years later.

By our standards as sixteen-year-olds, Doreen and Sheldon had been dating for a long time—over three months. His parents had met Doreen a couple of times and liked her, but they were upset that Sheldon was going out with a shiksa, a non-Jewish girl. They were afraid that he would marry her and forget all about being Jewish, maybe not even raise the kids Jewish. They needed a daughter-in-law who would light the Sabbath candles on Friday night, cook the Passover seder meals, get the children to Hebrew school every Tuesday evening and Sunday morning. It was understandable. They talked to Sheldon, he shared with Doreen, and the four of them all worried, maybe not about the same things. Doreen and I often talked about how torn she felt between wanting to stay with Sheldon and not wanting to upset his parents. It was important to her for everyone to be okay. So she cooked up her plan and asked Sheldon for help and he felt it was worth a shot. Then they pitched the plan to me. They'd set up a double date, with the other couple being me and Sheldon's best friend Joe, who was Jewish. Sheldon would tell his parents about the double date, and the parents would relax, because Sheldon was not the only Jewish boy in town going out with a shiksa.

Sheldon talked to Joe, who said he had seen me around our high school and I seemed like a nice girl, so he was fine with taking me out. I didn't know if Sheldon had told Joe the plan.

If I were smart enough to write a book on logic, I'd have put Doreen's plan in the same section of the book as Sheldon's claim that a lot of trayf chicken is trayf, but a little trayf chicken is still kosher. I couldn't figure out how, through the eyes of Sheldon's parents, two shiksas would be better than one. I thought they might worry even harder than before, because then not only Sheldon's future kids, but also Joe's, might not be raised Jewish. In fact, they might become afraid that intermarriage was taking over the world. Also, if you looked at it a different way, what if Joe and I didn't click, and we only went out together the one time? How would that show Sheldon's parents that it was a trend for Jewish boys to go out with shiksas?

So the way I saw it, the plan had plenty of holes.

Still, I appreciated the experience I was getting out of this date. Joe was okay, but I wouldn't be thinking of him all night long while kissing my pillow. If he were to ask me out again, I might say yes, but if he never did, I wouldn't be broken-hearted. I didn't have much of a past as a dater, and realized I had some catching up to do. The one boy I had gone out with more than three times was Glen Howard, who had split up with me after I beat him at arm-wrestling.

"Oh, Irene, I'm so mixed up," Doreen said.

"Why? What's going on?"

She cried again, and I got back into the comforting routine. Then she pulled away from me and gazed at the tile floor for a long time. The tiles were bite-sized white hexagons with heavy black borders. I looked at them for a few seconds and got dizzy, so I raised my head and waited.

Finally she looked up, "What a mess," she said. "I'm a big phony."

"No, you're not," I say.

"I am," she said. "I lied to you."

What was she talking about? We always told each other the truth.

"Me and Sheldon—the double date—the plan—"

I could have helped her to relax, so that her words wouldn't have such a hard time coming out, but instead I just stood by the sink with my arms folded. She'd have to recover the power of speech on her own. She had just warned me that she was about to say something I wouldn't be happy about, and I was in no rush to hear it.

It turned out that when Doreen had first thought up the plan, she was crazy about Sheldon, but that wasn't how she felt now. For the past two weeks, she had been wanting to break up with him. She still thought he was a nice guy, only she wasn't attracted to him any more. Not even a little.

"When he kisses me, I have to think about something else," she said.

"Like what? Another boy?"

"Not always. Just…anything. The Cuban heels I saw last week at Eaton's. A 7 Up float. A geometry proposition."

"What? You think about math while you're making out with him?"

She nodded.

"Okay, I'm trying to picture this. Sheldon is hot and bothered, he's sticking his tongue halfway down your throat, and you're thinking, *the square of the hypotenuse of a right-angled triangle is equal to—*"

"Stuff like that can come in handy when you're in an icky french kiss," she said.

We stood in silence for a moment. Then we both burst out laughing.

"So, why did you still want to go through with your plan?" I ask.

"I figured if *you* were here, we'd all have fun, and the four of us would stay together late. Midnight would roll around—my curfew. No time for a make-out session. What a shame. Then, when Sheldon took me to my door, I could quickly tell him it's over and dash into the house."

"So that's your Plan B," I said, and we laugh again. How could I be mad at her? This new plan was a lot more interesting than the old one.

When we returned to the table, it had been cleared. I had lost my appetite, and Doreen had never been interested in eating, so having the food gone was no loss. I didn't have to look at Joe's meal any more and was feeling okay about letting the evening play out.

"You know what goyish is?" Sheldon asked.

"Non-Jewish," I said.

"Correct," he said. "My mother told me there's a goyish superstition that if kids eat brains, they get smarter," he said.

My stomach turned. Joe laughed. "Come on, Irene. It's funny," he said.

I wanted to go home. Doreen pursed her lips. She looked like a girl determined to get her independence back before the night was out.

But she and Sheldon didn't split up that night. She couldn't bring herself to have the talk with him. They continued dating for two more months, until his father got transferred and his family moved to Toronto. For thirty-eight more petting sessions—she counted—Doreen kept busy solving algebra problems and buying shoes in her head.

Three weeks after the brains incident, Joe asked me out again. Partly out of pity and partly out of curiosity, I said yes. He took me to see Vincent Price in "The Red Masque of Death" at the Rialto on Park Avenue, and cracked his fingers through the whole show, until I was ready to amputate his hands. Meanwhile, on screen, we were treated to scenes of devil worship and bubonic plague.

He shouldn't have tried to kiss me.

Inservice

Who wants to choose

IN A WAY IT isn't Glenys's fault, she has just been in the game too long, she's lost her grip. Her confusion takes up a lot of space in the classroom, she can go ballistic over a tissue on the floor, an unlaced shoe.

Our ten-year-old Max starts wetting his pants, cries uncontrollably on a Friday night about the mistakes he made on his math test. I write a letter to Glenys, fill her in, ask to see her right away. Then I wait. And wait. And don't hear back.

Don't I owe it to that kid to take the problem to the principal?

Glenys taught Ian eleven years ago, no problem, he loved her. But once Max got her she had lost it, her craziness made the kid sick. I'm no sage, I'm no god, who wants to choose between Glenys and Max?

Three strikes you're out

Max is going to miss the morning bell again. A good kid but an up-and-down worker, late riser.

When we get to the side door of the school, the one by the playground, we hear a kid crying and Glenys yelling.

HOW MANY TIMES DO YOU THINK SORRY IS GOING TO WORK JASON SORRY DOESN'T CUT IT ANY MORE THIS IS THE THIRD TIME NOW SEE ME AFTER SCHOOL FOR LINES JASON YOU'RE GOING TO WRITE SO MANY LINES THAT BY THE TIME YOU FINISH YOU'LL HAVE AS MANY LINES ON YOUR FACE AS I DO IS THAT CLEAR JASON?

I decide to take Max in through the main entrance in front of the school. We'll report him late to the school secretary and he can sneak into class before Glenys returns; maybe she won't notice he's late.

Principal's office

The principal says, What is the reason you didn't answer the letter? The principal writes constantly in a coilbound scribbler. Glenys has the letter in her lap. I never wanted to write that letter. Dear Glenys, Please can we meet at your earliest convenience, Max is so anxious about school he has started bedwetting.

Glenys says she doesn't know why she didn't answer. Maybe, she says, maybe it's because the letter is so darn formal. At Your Earliest Convenience, we don't talk to each other that way, do we? I thought we were friends, Glenys says.

The principal says, You didn't answer because of the use of the phrase At Your Earliest Convenience?

Or maybe I forgot to answer, Glenys says, I'm a teacher, I've got a lot on my plate.

Glenys sucks at a hangnail on her right thumb, drifts

off, goes into a long stare at the wall.

The principal writes.

Kinder memories during the silence: Ian at ten, Glenys his teacher, Glenys right on the ball. I'm pregnant with Max, three days away from delivering by planned Caesarean. Agonizing over whether Ian will feel left out. I can't see bringing him into the operating room but I want him to feel that he's an important part of a big event. Glenys has the answer. Just get your hubby to phone the school Friday morning right after the C-section and ask for Ian. The secretary will page him over the intercom, your hubby will give him the news then and there, Ian will be in the know, the whole family will feel better.

Friday, Ian walks back into class after his father's call, Glenys asks, What's the scoop? He tells her, It's a boy. She leaves the room for a couple of minutes, comes back with paper plates and glasses, chocolate cake and pop. Glenys and the kids spend half an hour celebrating Max's birth with Ian.

Inservice

It's a science inservice, a training session to do with the new curriculum. Glenys has to go, the principal has a thing about professional development.

The inservice is scheduled for after school at the other end of the city. Glenys and the principal carpool, the principal teaches science too. It is not a wonderful seminar. Glenys would rather be at home with a murder mystery.

The next morning, early, the principal invites her into

the office and says, What did you think of the inservice?

Not bad, Glenys says. Nothing too exciting though.

Boring enough to put a person to sleep? the principal asks.

Silence.

Glenys looks at the principal. Did I snore? she asks.

That's not the point, the principal says.

Oh God, Glenys says.

Retreat

Today when I pick up Max after school, Glenys is good. My new word for lucid. Good. She tells me she convinced two other aging teachers (The Over Twenty-one Crowd, she calls them) to drive up to the mountains with her last Friday for the long weekend. We hiked in the day, she says, then we read in the evening, then damned if we could sleep, we stayed up on the Saturday night and again on the Sunday chewing the fat right into the wee hours.

She is buoyant as she tells the story, completely with it. Shades of eleven years ago.

The next day when I come to pick up Max she is staring out the window, not responding to any of the kids' goodbyes as they leave for the day. I greet her. Not a look, not a word.

Wedding

Ian is best man at his best friend Jay's wedding. The boys met in Glenys's grade five class. Now they're twenty-one. To Jay this means commitment, marriage, settling down.

To Ian it means he's of legal drinking age just about everywhere.

At the reception Ian sits with Glenys. The boys have kept in touch with her through the years, that's how good she used to be.

After the meal Glenys gets into the red wine in earnest. Her mauve lipstick has worked its way into the deep smoker's furrows around her mouth. She stares out at the dance floor. Ian says, what are you looking at, and she says, Legs. 1943. Nylon is at a premium, it's all going into the war effort, you can't buy stockings, you have to paint your legs and then draw seams down the back. Some girls use a paintbrush but personally I prefer an eyebrow pencil. You've got to be careful how you handle that pencil. You want exactly the right width to make that seam look like real. You have to keep moving straight up the centre, you can't be put off by the contours of the calf muscle.

She leans down, runs her right index finger along the back of her thin leg, ankle to thigh. The right side of her purple rayon skirt bunches up under her finger.

Ian takes a sip of water, clears his throat, consults his watch.

Damn, Glenys says, another run.

Announcement

Two weeks after the meeting at the principal's office Glenys announces that in September she will retire. I ask her what will you do. I'll learn to cut my own hair, she says. I'll read Grace Paley stories over and over. I'll take up bowling, join an Over Twenty-One team. I'll buy a gabardine wool blazer for tournaments, a stylish cut, nobody's going to make me put on one of those awful windbreakers. I'll bake three hundred and eleven Christmas cookies and bring them to the school, one for each kid, and anyone who tries to sneak seconds will be sorry. I'll make them write lines.

Casablanca

Our favourite rep theatre, The Roxy, shows Casablanca, we take Max, so few opportunities to see the classics on the big screen. In the lobby we bump into Glenys. She keeps calling Max by his brother Ian's name. The first time I correct her, then I let it go.

At the concession stand we wait in line behind Glenys. She orders a small popcorn, no butter, gives the young clerk a twenty, asks for her change in twos. The clerk scoops the popcorn into the container, places it in front of Glenys onto the counter, counts out into her hand eight two dollar coins and small change.

Glenys turns red, warms up, throws the change onto the counter. I WANT TWO DOLLAR BILLS REAL TWOS PROPER TWOS I DIDN'T ASK FOR BOARD GAME TOKENS.

The clerk reaches into his till and hands back her twenty dollar bill.

Your popcorn is on the house tonight, he says.

Kishkas

"YOU NEED TO CALL Howard and get a checkup right away," Alec says. "Not the slam-bam-thank-you-ma'am kind. A thorough physical."

"What is it?" Bernice asks.

"It's something with your kishkas," Alec says.

Bernice has never had problems with her intestines but she follows up immediately. A malignant polyp is found in her duodenum and excised. As far as the doctors can determine, the cancer has not spread.

"Alec knew about this one," Bernice tells Howard Gelfand.

"I see," Howard says quietly. As a matter of policy, he gives a low-key response when Bernice and Alec reveal their diagnoses of each other. Howard does not want to appear unprofessional, which is why he conceals his ongoing amazement at the couple's abilities to intuit each other's medical problems. For the fifteen years he has been their family doctor, they have been bang on every time. Alec knew Bernice was developing osteoarthritis in the joints of her left hand before she developed any symptoms. Bernice knew Alec needed prostate surgery when tests were still showing nothing.

Bernice and Alec discover their affinity for each other as soon as they meet. They first see each other in a bookstore in 1962. They spontaneously start talking. Almost forty years later they are still carrying on the conversation, still completely taken with each other. They have never consciously put work into their relationship. It grows naturally.

A year after they meet, Bernice moves into Alec's fourth floor walk-up. Her parents are appalled. She points out that she is thirty years old but they tell her there is no age limit in such matters. Bernice's father has a talk with Alec to ask him if his intentions are honourable. Alec says he and Bernice object to marriage on principle and in any event they do not intend to have children, so why bother with a meaningless ceremony. The father is not pleased with Alec's responses.

After that, Bernice has no further contact with her family.

As for Alec, who grew up in an Ottawa orphanage, he does not like to discuss his past. Bernice feels no compulsion to ask him about it.

Alec's work as a transportation planner takes him all over the world. Bernice always goes with him. They spend time in Europe, South America, the Middle East. Bernice establishes an excellent name as a writer of travel and human interest articles. She works freelance, selling stories to high-profile magazines and newspapers.

In 1975 Alec leaves for a project in Dubai. For the first

time Bernice, who is suffering with a persistent flu virus, is unable to go with him. During their two months apart, Alec becomes so despondent he stops eating. Finally he gets medical help and goes on a course of anti-depressants. Back home, Bernice has trouble shaking the virus and then develops cluster headaches. She sleeps poorly too.

Once Alec returns, they both regain their health quickly. This is when they decide they will not put themselves through another separation.

Now, Bernice is sixty-eight; Alec, sixty-seven. They are travel-weary and Alec has retired from transportation planning. He has become an accomplished calligrapher, pen and ink artist and paper maker. He creates custom-made special occasion cards; he designs and produces covers for poetry chapbooks. Bernice writes a syndicated newspaper column, called *Methuselah's Snowboard*, profiling adventurers over age sixty-five. Recently, she has written about an eighty-seven-year-old skydiver and a ninety-one-year-old pool shark.

On a bleak November afternoon, Bernice drives to a suburban mall. Alec's birthday is coming up. She wants to buy him binoculars which will do the job without costing the earth. They have taken up bird watching.

She walks purposefully along the second floor of the mall, heading for an outdoor equipment store. A well-dressed young man in his late thirties runs up to her in a panic.

"My wife," he says. "She's collapsed."

Bernice feels she may be able to help. She and Alec have taken a one-day CPR course, because you never know. She follows the man across the mall and into the parking lot. She winces because it is a strain to move this quickly; the arthritis has affected her feet.

The man stops by a van. Bernice catches up and when she has reached the van he pushes her in and closes the door.

"Oh my God," she says, and at that moment she decides to leave her body.

When the man goes to trial, Bernice watches Alec watching the man. She feels Alec's thoughts and takes his hand.

After this is over, they are a little more tired, a little less energetic than before. There are more trips than usual to Howard Gelfand's office. They develop chronic insomnia. Now instead of merely intuiting each other's problems, they develop symptoms to go with the intuition. Bernice suffers from nasal congestion because of Alec's recurring sinus infections and Alec's joints ache from Bernice's arthritis. Howard Gelfand asks their permission to write them up for a gerontology journal.

Bernice is just beginning an interview at the home of a seventy-three-year-old heli-skier. She doubles over in pain. The heli-skier reaches out to help but Bernice pushes him away. Bernice collects herself and tells the heli-skier she will call him soon to reschedule. Then she drives home, speeding, to tell Alec he needs to see the doctor right away. On the way, she kicks herself for not phoning from the heli-skier's house, for not carrying a cellphone, for not stopping to call 911. She knows it's something with Alec's heart. As soon as she unlocks the apartment door, she finds him lying dead on the floor.

At the memorial service, Bernice makes a point of not crying. She and Alec have never liked to display their deepest emotions to the outside world. There will be no formal mourning period, no shiva. She and Alec have never gone in for that sort of thing.

Bernice is relieved she and Alec arranged years ago to give their bodies to science when the time came. That decision will make life less unbearable today. There will be no trek to the cemetery. She will not need to hear the morbid creak of the winch as the coffin is lowered. She and Alec had thought of all that.

Right after the service, Bernice heads home. She has declined all invitations. When she gets back to the apartment she realizes that, for the first time since the rape, she no longer occupies her body.

She spends nine nights in concerted effort. On the tenth night, she succeeds in dying in her sleep.

According to the autopsy, the cause of death is a brain aneurysm.

Matinée

ESTELLE LEANS INTO THE front door of Marjorie's Lingerie as though it were made of solid lead. She plods her way to the cash desk with brow furrowed, eyes wide, mouth sealed so tightly you can't see her lips, as she struggles to stifle her sobs.

"Hi there," I say cheerfully, stopping my work for an instant. Then I continue sorting our new ecobags by size.

For some reason, our environmentally friendly supplier, GaiAmie, sent them in a jumble, with random handles knotted together and sizes intermixed, and it's taken me half an hour to get the bags organized. I wonder if GaiAmie does that haphazard packing on purpose, to remind us how things are going here on earth, where captive polar bears live on Prozac and finally die of their bad nerves.

Estelle likes to let on she's suffering in her mind too, but I've watched her make her entrance many times, and I can tell the difference between pain and performance. Every three weeks or so, in mid-afternoon, she comes to see me here at the store, and puts on a one-woman show. I do my best to keep my distance, but I've got a problem that keeps coming up.

"Irene, Penny is in terrible trouble," she says.

"Oh no."

There it is. Two seconds into today's conversation, my problem has surfaced again. I understand what she's doing and how she's doing it—and I am not a fan of her style—but still she drags me into her personal theatre, plunks me into a seat so close to the stage I can hear her breathe. She knows I care about Penny, who is also a customer—one who actually buys lingerie here, and also brightens my day every time she comes in. With an opening line I can't ignore, Estelle has sucked me in.

"What's wrong?" I ask. I place the medium ecobags on the lower shelf of the cash desk, and look up.

"She's engaged to a thirty-year-old guy," Estelle says.

What? It's not personal bankruptcy or a malignant polyp? An engagement is the big problem? For some people, it might be, but probably not for a level-headed woman like Penny.

"Is he a solid person?" I ask.

She goes quiet. It's a good sign. Through my questions I can sometimes get Estelle to think, even if only a little. In a couple of beats, she's back.

"I guess he's okay. It's just his age."

"Why not trust Penny's judgment?" I ask.

"What do you mean? She's still my kid."

I don't claim to understand what it's like to be a parent, although I care strongly for my young friend Julie. But I don't see how any mother of an adult child can be as tuned out as Estelle. Even my customer Paula, who tries to push around her grown daughter Renata, doesn't match Estelle for cluelessness. Estelle's whole attitude to Penny bothers me. Worry, misgivings, fear—that's all I hear about from Estelle. And how has Penny caused her mother aggravation? By working as a licensed practical nurse in a palliative care ward? By playing in a community volleyball league? Besides, Penny is a woman you just feel good to be around. She gives off the love-of-life energy people get from working with the dying.

But Estelle takes no pride in her daughter's achievements. As far as she is concerned, Penny's life is a tragedy, simply because she has never married. You'd think that with this engagement news, Estelle would finally be happy. But she refuses.

"How old is Penny now?" I say. "Mid-forties?"

"Forty-six on February twelfth."

"Okay then, you're talking about a person who's been alive for almost half a century," I say. "By now she knows her way around."

"He may be trying to take advantage of her."

"Where's the proof? Does he have a criminal record? Is he a con artist?"

"He's a fire fighter. But you'd think he'd go after a younger woman."

"Why? Maybe he's interested in Penny as a person, not in what date is written on her birth certificate."

"Well…I have to admit, he's done some nice things for her."

Silence. She may be thinking again.

"Can you give me an example?"

"Like when she decided to have her three-legged cockapoo Charlotte put to sleep. A few months after they amputated the bad leg, the cancer came back. They offered chemo but Penny said no. By then Charlotte was sad, sleeping all the time, not eating. And seeing as Penny puts such stock in quality of life, she made her decision."

"So how did the boyfriend help?"

"Brad?"

Good. She is finally showing the daughter-snatcher enough respect to mention his name.

"Well," she says, "he went with Penny when she took Charlotte for the last walk in River Park, and later he sat with her at the vet clinic and put his arm around Penny's shoulder as Charlotte sat in her lap and got the go-to-sleep shot. And he sat up with Penny all night and comforted her while she cried."

"All right," I say, as I hold a small ecobag up against the wall behind the cash desk, to see if that would be a good place to display our new earth-friendly packaging option. "So Brad is good to her and she's happy with him. Is that right?"

"That's the trouble," she says, lowering her voice, in case I didn't get it that this is a drama.

"Look," I say, "people don't get twisted up in knots over age differences any more. It doesn't matter. Besides, the way the planet is headed, we're all rocketing toward extinction pretty quick. So what's a sixteen-year gap between friends?"

"Plus, he lived with another woman for five years," she says, and looks at me for a big reaction.

"So what?" I say. "Who doesn't have a past?"

A real customer enters the store. I excuse myself, leave Estelle and go to help the new arrival. We've been through this scenario many times in the many years Estelle has been coming to Marjorie's Lingerie. Sometimes she leaves when I get busy with a customer; other times, she hangs around. I go about my business, and if she decides to stay, I get back to her when I can.

As soon as the customer leaves, I get on with sizing our boxed bras. We're running forty percent off on them this week and they've been picked over plenty, so the ones that are left are in disarray.

Estelle is still here. She stands next to me looking pained as I place the Playtex 4693s in the correct order by back measurement, cup size, and colour. It's amazing how much of a retail job involves setting things straight.

"So what'll I do about Penny?" Estelle whines.

"I don't see that it's up to you to do anything. She's an adult. We've discussed that."

But Estelle won't leave or give me peace until I find a way to reach her. Her thinking is so circular it makes me dizzy; I can only imagine what it does to her. And she is counting on me to stop her mental merry-go-round. I decide to do what my mother did when I was stuck on a problem: use an example, preferably from the British side of the family.

"You know," I say, "even in the twentieth century, the

royal family was still trying to control who their kids married. And just look at the results."

"You're thinking of Charles and that poor young Diana," Estelle says.

"Not to mention Princess Margaret."

"What happened to her?"

"I thought you might remember, but it's really not fair of me to assume that. After all, as a little girl, I heard about the royal family more than a lot of other people did, because my mother felt so close to them."

"Oh, everybody admired royalty in those days," Estelle says.

"True, but for her, it was personal. It started when she was expecting me, and Princess Elizabeth was expecting Prince Charles. My mother felt as though she and Elizabeth were sisters who happened to be going through pregnancies at exactly the same time. Charles and I were born within two days of each other."

"Gosh, it sure won't be easy for you to find a new husband at your age," Estelle says.

That's the mentality I am dealing with in Estelle. Now, I need to call on patience, which serves me so well in work and life.

"I'll be fine," I tell her. "Let's concentrate on the Windsors. When King George died, his daughters were crushed. Elizabeth had to pull herself together fast. Of course, she had her young family to take care of, and now she was also a queen, with a whole commonwealth to head up. She didn't have the luxury to get stuck in mourning. But poor Margaret had nothing to distract her from grief. Who could blame her for wanting…comfort?"

"You mean like, a man?"

"That's what I mean, yes."

"I just don't remember any of this," Estelle says.

No surprise there, I feel like saying. *No doubt you were wrapped up in yourself then, just like you are now. You have probably never had the listening energy to take in world events.*

"She started dating a much older guy named Peter Townsend," I say. "An aviator. He'd been a Spitfire pilot during the Second World War. A group captain. A war hero who'd fought in the Battle of Britain. In the 1950s, he and Margaret got together and my mother said this was it; for Margaret, he was the one. My mother had good instincts about the situation, because of course, in a way, she and Margaret were sisters."

"Sisters? How's that?" Estelle asks.

I'm thinking, *Come on, Estelle, you can do it. You can connect the dots. Put that brain of yours to work.* But she doesn't want to, so I will leave it to her to wake up in bed at three o'clock tomorrow morning and ponder the puzzle of the three sisters. It'll be a good mental exercise for her.

"The Windsors weren't pleased. First of all, Townsend was a commoner and divorced. But what bugged them even more was his age," I say. "Even today I can't figure out what their problem was. If people are grownups, they should be left alone in such matters. That's what I think and it's what my mother thought too. But the Windsors had different ideas. Plus Townsend had baggage—he had been married. And some people even thought Margaret had been involved with him before his divorce came through."

"A princess would never behave like that," Estelle says.

"She really wanted to marry Townsend but her family set impossible conditions."

"Like what?"

"Well, I'm not sure I remember exactly what my mother told me, so don't sue me if a get some details wrong."

"I haven't got the stomach for lawsuits," Estelle says.

"They read her the Riot Act. If you marry him, kiss your living allowance goodbye, lose your place in line for the throne, forget about a church wedding. Oh, and get the heck out of town."

"What, they were going to throw her out of her own home?"

"They wanted her to leave the country for five years. They felt the English people would need time to adjust to the idea of sharing space with such a wicked princess."

"So what did she do?"

"Well, I imagine she had some tough thinking sessions that went on for hours at a time. In the end, she gave Townsend up, and she said it was her decision, but my mother was sure it was the family pressure that did it."

"Well, after a while, I'm sure she got over him," Estelle

says.

It makes me crazy when people rewrite history to suit their own purposes. Even with all my years of retail experience, I can't stay patient forever.

"How does a person get over the love of her life?" I say. "Oh, she tried to do what was right. A few years after the breakup, she married a photographer with a hyphenated name. Anthony Something-Something. Tony."

"So then, everything worked out fine."

"Not so fast, Estelle. They weren't exactly the perfect couple. Tony chased a lot of skirt, and also went after men. Margaret was no angel in the faithfulness department either. They fought. After close to twenty years of misery together, they divorced. She got two kids out of that marriage, but zero satisfaction. And she'd also gotten deeper into some lousy habits, out of frustration. Smoked non-stop, drank hard, never treated herself or her body properly for the rest of her life."

"Maybe she was like that," Estelle says.

"Like what?" I say.

"You know—the type that hurt themselves."

"She didn't start out that way, did she?" I say.

I excuse myself to serve another customer, who winds up needing help in a fitting room. When I emerge, Estelle is gone.

Why do I let her perform here at the store? She isn't a real customer; she's told me herself that she buys all her underwear at Zeller's. I have no duty as a professional to give her my time. In fact, it would probably be more responsible for me to kick her out when she shows up, because she distracts me.

Do I listen because I care about her? How can I, when she insists on making herself dumb? What's worse, she's often mean. A couple of years ago, I had it out with her when she ran around town maligning my friend Reuben. I told her to cut out the badmouthing pronto, and I didn't make any effort to soften my message. I thought Estelle and I were done for good, but a few weeks later she was back, going on about something else.

Is it for Penny's sake that I bother with Estelle? That can't be. I play no part in what passes between mother and daughter.

Maybe I put up with Estelle as a way of doing something for a person less fortunate than me. I mean, as humans, we're supposed to reach out that way. What's less fortunate about Estelle though? She assumes too much, won't look at a situation from another person's point of view, doesn't use her head enough. She has never cultivated the art of listening. Does all that shabby behaviour make her less fortunate, or just irritating?

I've got to face up to it, Estelle has something to offer me. Otherwise, I'd end it, even if that took some doing and made me feel awful. I've never been one to let a bad thing go on out of laziness. She gives me something more than cheesy entertainment. But what?

* * *

In the middle of the night I wake up thinking, suppose Margaret were to rise from the dead and have a few words with Estelle. "Look here, missus, if you don't leave your daughter alone, she may drop Brad, but then she will take more lovers than you would care to know about, and none will be the cream of the crop either. She will die before you do, out of heartache, hard living, and spite. She will choose to be cremated because you'd rather that she be buried. Meanwhile, Brad will marry a woman who looks just like Penny—and how will that make you feel?"

My goodness. I didn't know Auntie Margaret had such a mouth on her.

Acknowledgments

It is hard to do acknowledgments because of the fear of forgetting someone. So the first thing I want to acknowledge is my error, if I have left anybody out. Believe me, the omission is unintended. Also, some names belong in more than one paragraph but I have mentioned each only once, in order to avoid sounding like I am making an acceptance speech at the Academy Awards. Except for the family paragraph, names appear alphabetically.

Family sustains me. Bill Paterson, Irwin Altrows, Grace Paterson, Lucy Altrows, Simon Evans and Oliver Evans, this book exists because of you.

Friends who also write fiction help me stay strong. Maureen Bush, Lori Hahnel, and Naomi K. Lewis, thanks for standing by me and for being such pros.

The right editor is indispensible. Thank you, Dustin Smith, for a perceptive and democratic edit.

I am grateful for the camaraderie, listening capacity and comfort of other friends and colleagues, too. Some write, and some do other worthwhile things with their lives (because apparently, that is a valid choice). Thank you to Joseph Bardsley, Susan Calder, Sharon Cavanagh, Tim Christison, Ethan Cole, Shirley Dunn, Susan Farmer, Leslie Gavel, Diane Girard, Genevieve Graham-Sawchyn, Marion Gauzer, Eleanor King Byers, Jan Markley, Elaine Morin, Marion Nichols, Lori D. Roadhouse, Roberta Rees, Lori Shyba, Inge Trueman, Jenny Tzanakos, and Marje Wing.

I am indebted to the Calgary Public Library; the Alexandra Writers' Centre Society and its program co-ordinator Robin van Eck; and the Canadian Authors Association. Each has trusted me to be Writer-in-Residence at some point during the writing and production of *Key In Lock*. Samantha Warwick and The Writers' Guild of Alberta have also shown me a good deal of support.

Thank you to the Canada Council for the Arts and the Alberta Foundation of the Arts for supporting the creation of this book through the Alberta Creative Development Initiative.

Earlier versions of *Key In Lock* stories have appeared in magazines, anthologies and e-zines. Thank you to the editors of these publications: *blue buffalo, Contemporary Verse 2, Dandelion, Fireweed, mixed messages, Montreal Serai, Other Voices, The Prairie Journal of Canadian Literature,* and *Ryga, A Journal of Provocations*. Some of these publications have carried more than one of the stories in *Key In Lock*.

The CBC produced "Briefing Notes" on radio, and Image Theatre staged "Duck for Cover, Joan." I am grateful to both.

I am so grateful to the great Gabriel von Max for creating the work *Woman in Contemplation* and to Jack Daulton for generously endorsing my use of that work on the book cover.

Finally, I want to thank Recliner Books for its refreshingly progressive approach to publishing, and for taking a chance on me.